COLIN

BROTHERHOOD PROTECTORS WORLD

REGAN BLACK

Twisted Page Press LLC

BROTHERHOOD PROTECTORS

ORIGINAL SERIES BY ELLE JAMES

Brotherhood Protectors Series
Montana SEAL (#1)
Bride Protector SEAL (#2)
Montana D-Force (#3)
Cowboy D-Force (#4)
Montana Ranger (#5)
Montana Dog Soldier (#6)
Montana SEAL Daddy (#7)
Montana Ranger's Wedding Vow (#8)
Montana SEAL Undercover Daddy (#9)
Cape Cod SEAL Rescue (#10)
Montana SEAL Friendly Fire (#11)
Montana SEAL's Mail-Order Bride (#12)
Montana Rescue (Sleeper SEAL)
Hot SEAL Salty Dog (SEALs in Paradise)
Brotherhood Protectors Vol 1

With special thanks to Elle James for inviting me into her world of Brotherhood Protectors.

GUARDIAN AGENCY: COLIN

ABOUT *GUARDIAN AGENCY: COLIN*

When hope is lost, truth is blurred, and your life is on the line,
it's time to call in the Guardian Agency...

He's ex-Army. She's a witness in danger. Together they must fight the ghosts of the past to survive the killer on her trail.

Summer Curley is on the run after her witness-protection detail is gunned down. With no one to trust, she can only hope that hiding will buy her enough time to make a plan.

Colin Hazard's Army career ended after weeks as a prisoner of war. Now he finds purpose as a body-guard and when he's assigned to locate and protect an important witness, he dives into action.

But keeping Summer safe is only the first problem. Colin soon learns the case and the woman are far more complex than he expected. Between her secrets and the ghosts of his past, staying alive could mean sacrificing his heart.

Visit ReganBlack.com for a full list of books, excerpts and upcoming release dates.
For early access to new releases, exclusive prizes, and much more,
subscribe to Regan's monthly newsletter.

CHAPTER 1

COLIN HAZARD'S cell phone chimed. He finished his last set of pushups and flopped to his back, his shoulders shaking. He reached blindly, his hand skimming the edge of the weight bench until he found his phone.

There was one message and only one word: PROTECT

The one word didn't surprise him. As a bodyguard with the Guardian Agency, that was his job. The timing felt suspect. Rushed. Forced. He'd just wrapped up a case that tripped a few of his hot buttons and he needed the downtime. Naturally, he hadn't broadcast the struggle. He'd kept the client safe and come home to work off the residual effect.

Did they think he was a machine, or was the agency afraid he'd go rogue again if they didn't keep him in the field?

He paused and breathed through the misplaced frustration, concentrating on the reality rather than the memories clawing at him. He was overthinking the situation, assigning opinions and biases to people who probably weren't thinking about him at all, beyond his skills as an employee.

So what if he'd just wrapped up a case and hit send on his final report less than twenty-four hours ago? The lawyers, Gamble and Swann, who'd offered him a post with this investigation and protection service had made his role clear. His job was to respond to the call whenever it came through. Didn't matter that he'd never had back-to-back cases before.

With the phone in his hand, he rolled to his feet, bouncing on his toes like a boxer and rolling his shoulders. "Today's a new day," he said to the mirrored wall, using his psychiatrist's words.

He studied his reflection with a critical eye, trying to decide if he liked the view today.

In general, he could look at himself and find the familiar. The red hair, the freckles dusting his pale skin, and the squared off jaw all felt normal. There were the scars, old and new, some of them triggering scarred-over memories better left undisturbed. The eyes... he looked away from his reflection. What kind of fool stared at his own eyes when there was work to do?

Back-to-back cases might not be the norm, but

clearly he needed the distraction more than he realized.

Stripping off his shorts, he showered quickly and dressed while he waited for the details on the case to come through. The next alert from the phone wasn't a text or even an email with a file attached. It was an incoming call from Gamble and Swann.

"Mr. Hazard." A woman's voice greeted him, precise Ivy League education winding through it. "You're needed in Eagle Rock, Montana for a face-to-face briefing for your new case."

Montana? Seriously? And he'd never heard of Eagle Rock. The lawyers had parked him in Denver, Colorado and told him this would be his region. He preferred the city, the mountain views, and the options for day trips and weekend getaways when he needed the space. "All right. I can be on the road within ten minutes."

"A private plane will be waiting for you at Denver International."

His jaw clenched. Planes sucked. Tiny planes were worse. He couldn't imagine an airfield in a town he'd never heard of equipped for a substantial aircraft big enough to hold its own against wind and weather.

"No time for me to drive?"

"Not unless we delay the briefing."

Clearly that wasn't ideal. Warning bells sounded in his head, not unlike the alarms on a plane falling from the sky. "Is the client in Denver?"

"Details will be provided at your meeting."

So what they needed to share they didn't trust to phone calls. Interesting. Now, his curiosity was in high gear. "Guess I'm headed to the airport."

"Thank you. Further instructions will come through shortly," she said and then disconnected.

He tucked the phone into his pocket and went to grab his gear. All of this felt like a colossal waste of time, but he wasn't the man in charge anymore. Didn't want to be. He'd learned the hard way that leadership carried a heavy, nearly unbearable price.

He grabbed his overnight bag and held a brief debate over the handgun and knife he carried most of the time. He had the training, experience and permits for both. Hopefully a private plane meant bypassing typical security hoops.

Now he was wasting time. He had to get to the meeting before he could make any sort of educated guess about the assignment or how it would go down. Locking up his condo, he took the stairs to the garage.

He tossed his duffle, weapons included, into the trunk of his Audi R8 coupe before sliding into the driver's seat. Once there, the first layer of tension eased off his shoulders. Control and power rested under his hands, under the hood of this flawless machine. He started the engine, soaking up the comfort and rush. His shrink had encouraged this, called it an investment.

An investment in sanity, Colin thought, backing out of his parking space.

The call came through, his hands-free system announcing Tyler, the agency-assigned tech and research assistant he'd never met personally.

"What's going on, Ty?"

"We've got an all hands on deck, Col," the other man mimicked his tone perfectly. "You're departing from the private charters flight terminal. I've sent the directions to your navigation app. You won't have to worry about security lines."

"Thanks." He swallowed his opinion of flying on a small plane all the way to Montana. He wasn't sure skipping the lines was worth it. He looked at the sky, hoping there weren't any storms out there waiting for him. "Where is Eagle Rock anyway?"

"Foothills of the Crazy Mountains."

"Never heard of those," Colin admitted.

"You will soon enough," Tyler muttered. "The case is tricky," he continued. "And time sensitive."

"Aren't they all?" Colin deadpanned. "If there's such a rush, why fly me out for a briefing? We couldn't have done this online or with a conference call while I'm en route?"

"No. This time around no one has much faith in the security of standard communication."

That was actually more distressing than flying. Guardian Agency had the best secured network he'd ever seen and he'd worked some highly confidential operations during his military time. "Fine."

"Safe travels," Tyler said, ending the call.

His assistant should probably give that sentiment to the flight crew. Thanks to his control issues, Colin wasn't the best passenger in any type of vehicle, but airplanes were especially harrowing.

He cringed when he reached the airport and passed rows of small aircraft on his way to the designated terminal. To his shock, the capable-looking, sleek corporate jet on the tarmac was waiting for him. He hadn't seen the inside of one of these since... He had to swallow the annoying surge of emotion. Since just before his final deployment with the U.S. Army.

His dad had surprised him, flying in to take him to the Indianapolis 500 for one last weekend before his unit deployed.

That trip had been a whirlwind of color from the clear blue sky to the logo-ed up cars on the track. Sounds of engines and fans. The pre-race spectacle and the race itself. The scents of the hot track, soft rubber, and the raw power as the drivers circled the track, vying for the lead.

He'd had no idea that singular day, the memory symbolic of everything he stood for would become his touchstone, his lifeline when the mission went to hell.

Colin kept that trip front of mind now as he

boarded the plane and buckled into the luxurious leather seat. Once they were in the air, he opened his laptop and started combing news reports for information and insight about Eagle Rock.

No wonder he'd never heard of it. The place was tucked away, protected and isolated from the rest of the world. Remote was only part of the story. From the overhead pictures, sprawling ranches surrounded a smallish town that was hemmed in by a ridge of rugged mountains. Checking ranch names and ownership it seemed the rich and famous were turning this little pocket of privacy into their own western playground, he thought, reading on.

Great information, but so far, he was coming up dry on why this town should be in the news or what any of the names he could tie to the place mattered to the agency he worked for. Did they have a serial killer on the loose, he wondered, closing the laptop. In his short experience, the agency didn't seem to take those kinds of cases. But what else would necessitate the avoidance of standard communication. He'd know soon enough.

The jet landed and taxied well away from the runway and right up to an open hangar. He tossed his bag over his shoulder and tried to walk rather than run out of the aircraft. Luxury aside, it still amounted to being trapped in a can he couldn't escape.

A man waited for Colin inside the hangar, a cowboy hat shading his eyes. Despite the casual jeans, button-down shirt open at the collar, and clean boots, he had a physique and poise that telegraphed his ability to turn lethal at a moment's notice.

"Colin Hazard?"

"That's right," Colin replied.

The man didn't smile as he stuck out his hand. "Hank Patterson."

Colin nearly choked. He'd read through several reports detailing operations by Patterson and his SEAL team. He hadn't known the man had retired out here. This man couldn't possibly be in need of protection. What kind of SEAL—active or retired— would even accept a bodyguard?

"I run my own protective services agency these days," Hank said, leading the way to an office just off the hangar. "We're based here in Eagle Rock. Your group reached out to mine, the Brotherhood Protectors, as a precaution."

"For what?"

"A federal case being prosecuted in Helena has been jeopardized by what law enforcement generally refers to as the Native Mob."

Colin had never heard the term.

"They use it as a blanket term for general organized crime among the Native American population. The U.S. Attorney, Billie Hamilton, is prosecuting the case. She has ties to your agency, but I have local ties." Hank opened the door for Colin to enter the office. "This situation requires a delicate touch."

Colin, still a bit lost by the choices made by people above his pay grade, waited for more information. In his experience the person who spoke first often lost control of the conversation.

"Someone, presumably from the prosecutor's office, leaked intel," Hank said baldly. He handed over a plain manila file folder. "Three protected witnesses have been compromised. Full names, safe house locations, prior addresses and relations. Everything." He muttered an oath. "Another bodyguard from your agency found the first witness and has her secure now, but two more women remain missing. This is your assignment."

Colin opened the file. The pictures hit him like a sucker-punch. One head-shot style photo was paper clipped to a page of several candid photos of the woman in various activities. A picnic, at a school, and some formal event. A fundraiser or banquet of some sort. He usually received this intel on his computer. Holding it in his hands made his assignment even more real.

The woman was beautiful. Beyond beautiful. Her oval face was defined by high cheekbones, a straight nose and big dark eyes that stared right through him. She was more than his vocabulary could handle. A spark rippled through his bloodstream. It had been so long since *that* had happened, he was tempted to check his pulse.

He wasn't here as a model scout or in search of

the perfect date. No. Once he found her, he would be her bodyguard.

"Good collection of angles," he said, grasping for the ragged edges of his professionalism. "Where was," he flipped the folder and double checked the name, "Summer Curley last seen?"

"In Helena. Yesterday," Hank replied. "The security detail for another witness was shot and killed on the courthouse steps. Apparently, Summer's team cut her loose."

"Cut her *loose?*" That was about the worst thing he'd heard so far. "I sure as hell missed that as a tactic in the Protection 101 Manual."

Hank's scowl indicated he agreed with Colin. "From what I can piece together from the reports, her team was overwhelmed and it was a rash attempt to give her a head start," Hank explained. He motioned for Colin to turn the page. "Ms. Curley's detail was also killed in the line of duty."

Colin managed not to wince at the graphic photo, but he couldn't suppress the violent curse that slipped through his lips. He supposed a day that dead bodies didn't bother him was the day he should walk into the sunset and never look back.

"You've been asked to locate Ms. Curley and keep her safe and get her to the courthouse in one piece so she can testify. It's all in there. Everything we have on her ties to the case and her life prior to becoming a witness. If you need support locally or elsewhere, my team is here to help. We have all the assets you'd expect. Safe houses, radios. Backup."

Colin glanced up from the folder at that last word. Something in Patterson's tone put him on edge. His past was supposed to be a closed book. The escape and rendezvous with a patrol had made it into military news, but it had been heavily spun and the details cautiously redacted to protect the Army and everyone involved.

What did Hank know and how did he find out? Other than Gamble and Swann, no one at the Guardian Agency had the full details of his last Army operation and his struggle to become a civilian again. All of that was irrelevant. He was here about a woman in serious trouble. "I have an assistant," he said at last. "He and I have a good system."

"Tyler is excellent," Hank said. "We've spoken a few times since this mess blew up in Helena. He can always reach me. Cell phones and email are necessary, but remember they're also the least secure lines of communication until we find and plug the leak."

"You're sure she's alive?" Colin leaned over the open file folder while his mind whirled.

"Sure as we can be. Her body hasn't turned up." Hank folded his arms over his chest. "Your assistant and my team have been combing traffic cameras, social media, and everything else we can think of."

"With no leads yet?"

"Correct," Hank confirmed.

A lack of a body was some good news. Colin paged through the file, recognizing Tyler's thorough touch in the information presented. He didn't especially want to know how his assistant always managed to access the details that gave Colin such a superb picture of their clients.

This client, Summer Curley, was a full-blooded Crow Indian and she'd been born and raised on the reservation in Montana. She'd graduated high school with honors. In college she majored in secondary education, graduating at the top of her class with dual bachelor's and master's degrees. Prior to getting tangled up in this kidnapping case, she taught at a high school on another Indian reservation.

"Hang on," Colin said, as a detail caught his attention. "She's the *sister* of the primary victim in this case?"

Hank nodded, somberly. "Autumn Curley managed to escape her captors after the better part of two years. She did it right here in Eagle Rock. The two men traveling with her were arrested and have been in jail awaiting trial ever since. Reading between the lines in the reports shared with me, the girl has an uncanny memory. She gave up locations, names, and descriptions that exposed a major trafficking ring."

Colin whistled. The wheels in his head were spinning. He swore again as things clicked into place.

"You're saying Summer witnessed her sister's abduction?"

"Apparently."

Colin had seen more heartache than he cared to discuss and he'd survived some dreadful events, but that kind of trauma was new territory. "Why call me in? Ties or not between Hamilton and the Guardian Agency, your group is right here in the thick of it." He closed the file and tapped his fingertips against it. "By my guess everyone in your crew is as capable as you."

Hank's gaze narrowed and belatedly, Colin recognized his misstep. *Aw, hell.* That hadn't been a challenge, just an observation.

"What do you know of me or my crew?" Hank queried, folding his arms over his chest.

The man's voice was flat and far too neutral. Colin didn't twitch, held his ground. "In my time with the Army, I read about one or two of your SEAL team missions."

"Is that so?"

Now Hank was analyzing him for any insight into how and where he'd served. Very few people were allowed to view sensitive mission reports like those Patterson and his team had conducted. Once again Colin proved the lasting effectiveness of his PSYOP training.

"That's the extent of it," he confirmed. Hank was tough, but no one equaled Colin's ability to keep secrets buried. "A file crossed my desk a time or two.

I don't *know* your group at all. I can't claim to know anyone on your crew specifically," he added. "But you strike me as a man who prefers to work with like-minded men."

"And women."

"Even better." Colin offered up a tight smile. Hank relaxed a fraction. "Thank you for the intel. I'll take it from here."

He turned to leave and stopped. "One question." He watched Hank rock back on his heels, arms still folded. "Where do *you* think Summer would go?"

Hank tipped his hat back and shook his head. "Until this rash of women getting kidnapped off the reservations came to light, my guess would be that she'd head home. We have eyes on her house, the route to the house where she and her sister grew up, and her school. We'll contact Tyler if we spot her."

"Backup," Colin said, smiling at Hank's slight nod. "Thanks." It would be a huge help to have those obvious locations under surveillance. He was good, but he'd be hard pressed to find a Native American woman on rural land she would know how to navigate.

He reached out and shook Hank's hand. "You'll know when I have her secure and safe." Walking out of the office, he jogged back to the plane. Precautions or not, he felt as if they'd wasted too many hours bringing him up here.

Summer Curley could be anywhere by now, including dead on a street.

As he buckled into the seat and the pilot prepared for takeoff, he opened the file and applied his extensive training and PSYOP work to dredge up a clue as to where she might be hiding. His intuition had kicked into high gear and the hair on the back of his neck lifted. He needed to find her fast, before this Native Mob caught up with her.

CHAPTER 2

SUMMER CURLEY SCURRIED through downtown Denver, Colorado, unable to shake the knowledge that she'd been found. The sensation had more to do with logic than any superb intuition or hyper-awareness on her part. It wasn't even about paranoia, as if that mattered now. Since she wasn't ready to die, she needed to find a solution. Fast.

She ducked into the next store front and found herself in small grocery. Her stomach rumbled and she strolled along the first aisle, keeping an eye on the people moving along outside. No one out there seemed too interested in her or the store. At the counter, she purchased a candy bar with the little cash she had left. Trouble pressed in at the edges of her mind. She needed help, but who could she call? Anyone she involved would also become a target. That burden squashed her hunger as she timed her exit to coincide with another group of people passing by.

Statistics about safety in numbers held true time and again.

If the people who wanted her dead succeeded, would the authorities even put her death into the right column? An odd point to get hung up on, but her math and statistics teacher's brain couldn't help wondering. The details mattered, especially when the crucial detail was her life. It would be horrible to get killed and listed as a Jane Doe, one more victim of random violence.

Until her body was properly identified. Assuming the people on her trail left her body intact enough to make an identification. There were no guarantees for her, not anymore.

For months, she'd craved some space and alone time. Now all she wanted was one good person on her side, someone to watch over her for a few hours so she could really sleep. It had only been a day, but it felt longer since Marie, the woman in charge of her security team had gone pale and urged her to run.

They'd been enjoying an early lunch before Summer was scheduled to meet the prosecution team at the Helena, Montana courthouse for one last review of her testimony and what to expect when she testified. Summer had been riding a high of sweet anticipation knowing the men who had kidnapped her sister two years ago would soon get the justice they deserved.

Thirty seconds had been all the time needed to dash that high. One brief, tense phone call followed by the sudden appearance of a hired killer, and she was on the run, with no way to end this new nightmare. Her mind replayed it all again as she wandered down the street with no clear destination.

"Summer, you've been a trooper," her lead security officer said. *Marie had demonstrated kindness and common sense under the thick layer of steel-plated badass required to keep Summer safe. "Not many people would hold up so well."*

"You've made protective custody as nice as possible," *Summer replied.*

They'd become something akin to friends, after the initial adjustments. Summer had struggled mightily with the restrictions, missing her work and worrying over the students who would feel abandoned. The worst part was being boxed up in a non-descript house with little access to nature and no access to friends and family. Not that family had amounted to much since her sister's kidnapping.

"Almost over," *Marie said with a smile. "What's the first thing you'll do?"*

A long walk, followed by more basking in sunshine and nature. Maybe she'd take a drive through the reservation, windows down, radio up, stopping whenever the view stole her breath. She and her sister, Autumn, had done that countless times before...

She forced herself to think the words, to deliberately recall the horror of her sister's kidnapping. Soon enough she'd have to say it all out loud in front of strangers.

For some reason, the recollections were worse in her head than when she practiced her testimony. "I'll need to see my dad," Summer said. It wouldn't be anything as restorative as a walk or drive, despite her father's remote patch of land in a nearly inaccessible area of the Crow Reservation.

"He won't be at the trial?"

Summer shook her head. "I can't imagine him making the effort. What happened to my sister wrecked him," she murmured, ashamed of herself for judging him so harshly. "Do you think Autumn will be able to go home?" she asked instead.

Marie had lifted her water glass, and paused in that way she had of thinking before she spoke. "She's an enemy of the Native Mob. Your sister may have to change everything to survive."

An unsettling concept, knowing her sister. "So am I," Summer pointed out. "But you're letting me go home."

"It's different." Marie frowned. "You'll testify against two men for one particular incident. I don't know all of the particulars, but I believe your sister has offered up information that could bring down the entire trafficking operation."

Summer tried to be thankful that something good

would come out of the tragedy that shattered her family beyond any hope of reconciliation.

Marie started to say something more when the phone interrupted her. She answered, listening. Slowly the color leached from her face. "I'll call when we're reset," she said, tucking the phone into her pocket.

"Another witness was just attacked at the courthouse. Her security detail is dead." Marie reached into her purse, pulling out several hundred dollars. She shoved the money into Summer's hands. "It's all I have. Go to the bathroom and wait for me. If I don't come for you, leave through the back door and get as far from here as possible."

"What's wrong?"

"There's reason to believe someone is aiming for you too. Backup is on the way. Go on and hide."

"Let me help." Summer couldn't move. She didn't want to leave the woman who had become a friend. Couldn't bear to have more blood on her hands. "Marie—"

"Go, Summer. Now."

She obeyed, glancing back just long enough to watch Marie leave the table, her weapon drawn.

She'd seen Marie again several minutes later, life-less on the sidewalk, surrounded by chaos. The memory left her lurching forward and in her grief, she stumbled into a man waiting for the traffic light to change. "Watch it," he said, his lip curled in distaste.

She mumbled an apology, thinking of how disappointed Marie would be. Summer had fled from

Helena, but she was still in significant danger. Drawing any kind of attention was a mistake. The light changed and she crossed with the other pedestrians without incident.

From the bathroom of that restaurant, Summer had heard the brief exchange of gunfire and what felt like endless screams. Several women had crowded into the space, crying and asking questions. Eventually, someone pushed open the door and declared the crisis over. Summer flowed along with the crowd, exiting through the back door. She'd been across the street, stunned by the dreadful turn of events, when the police arrived and surrounded the block.

In the twenty-four hours that followed, she'd put as much distance as possible between herself and the restaurant in Helena. She didn't waste the cash on a motel room. She'd thrown away the phone Marie had given her at the beginning of her stay in protective custody. Pushing the terror from her mind, she'd walked to the nearest hotel and taken the next available shuttle to the airport. From there she'd found a cab to take her to the nearest truck stop.

At the truck stop, she'd purchased different clothing, including a ball cap. While sitting at the counter, hunched over a cup of coffee, she'd assessed the drivers coming and going. When the news program on the television in the corner flashed her face up next to a concerned anchorman, she bravely watched the report along with the strangers on either side of her.

Deciding who to ask for a ride had taken her a bit longer than intended after that tense moment, but she'd done it. Catching a ride with a barrel-chested bear of a man with a weathered face and a quick grin, she rode into Denver.

No one would look for her here. She'd only been in town as a tourist and once for a professional conference. And during those visits, she'd never been to this part of town. She was counting on the population to hide her, to blur her trail until she could figure out her next step. But someone had already found her.

Being a teacher, she knew everything in public was likely to get caught on some sort of camera. She'd been as careful as possible, keeping her head low as she'd worked her way out of Helena. Denver should've given her some anonymity, some space to regroup and come up with a plan. It had turned into a maze of danger with a killer closing in.

Not at all what she'd been hoping for.

Nervous again, she ducked into the next storefront, realizing too late it was a pawn shop. Cursing herself for the error, she wandered around the displays, again keeping an eye on the door and the flow of people outside.

A ginger-haired man strolled by, sunglasses on his face, his hands tucked into his pockets. Her intuition screamed in warning, though he hadn't even glanced at the pawn shop window.

Redheads were far more common than the proverbial unicorn, but she'd seen this particular man more than once today. And in this gritty part of town he stood out. The glossy hair, the clean boots, and the high-end sunglasses all indicated he had money, or knew where to buy convincing knockoffs to achieve his designer look.

None of the news articles or reports about the shooting in Helena had provided any helpful details about the shooter who'd killed Maric in an attempt to get to Summer. Apparently no one wanted to catch a killer, they were fixated on showing her face as a person of interest. It made her wonder whose side the media was on. She would've thought a U.S. Attorney intent on keeping a key witness alive would've had more pull about the flow of information.

"You buying or selling?" a deep voice boomed from behind her.

Her heart stuttered at the loud demand and she jerked around to face a large man filling the caged opening between Plexiglas panels that blocked off the back of the store. Knees wobbling, she ignored the question and turned back to the front window where several guitars were on display. She wasn't in the market for a guitar, but it bought her a moment to consider parting with anything of value on her person.

The money stashed in the lining of her purse wouldn't last forever and she still had no idea who to trust or where to turn. Going to the police seemed like a no-brainer but when she'd made her way to a Denver PD precinct, she'd chickened out. If Marie couldn't keep her safe, who could?

In the years before her sister had been kidnapped, she could've called on their father to come pick her up from any situation. Now she didn't dare. Not only had he slipped into a barely-there depression, he'd spat in the dirt and told her the world outside his farm didn't deserve his attention. When Roger Bodaway Curley spoke, there was no going back.

"Lady!" the man in the cage shouted again. "Buy something, sell something, or get the hell out of my store."

Her fingertips automatically went to the silver locket and chain she wore every day. Tears burned the backs of her eyes. The necklace was all she had left of her mother. A coil of her mother's dark hair and a tiny photograph. That, along with a turquoise bracelet and ring were the only valuables she'd taken with her into protective custody. She'd been wearing all three pieces yesterday, when she was forced to run for her life.

She glanced to the window and saw a non-descript man stride by. He looked in, met her gaze through the glass and kept going. A tremor rippled through her. She didn't want to sell and she didn't need to do so right this second, but going back out on the street held even less appeal.

"I'm just looking," she said to the man in the cage.

"That wasn't one of the options. Get out." He was big, with straight black hair pulled back from a round face. His almond-shaped eyes held a glint of barely-restrained meanness.

"Guess you don't live and die on reviews," she muttered.

He stood up and leaned menacingly close to the window. She was afraid, despite the layers of nicked-up Plexiglas and the sturdy wire-fence panel between them.

"Buy or sell something, little girl, and I'll show you service to write home about."

"Right." She backed toward the door. "Sorry to bother you." Her heel caught on a freestanding display of available silverware patterns and she tumbled back, her arms pinwheeling as she tried to keep from falling on the filthy floor.

Tried and failed. She landed on her butt, hard enough to make her eyes water. She didn't have time to cry. Not here, not when she'd just spotted a camera in the corner. She ducked her head, feeling like a toddler on the verge of a serious meltdown.

"You okay?" A strong, male hand appeared in front of her face.

She'd been too distracted to notice anyone else enter the shop. At this rate, she should just let the Native Mob take her out. Her odds of survival were negligible. Feeling defeated, embarrassed, and thoroughly frustrated, she clasped the offered hand. He pulled her to her feet and the momentum carried her right into his body.

Mistake! Her inner voice shrieked when she saw the knife he had aimed at her belly.

Something—someone—knocked her out of the way and she crashed into the silverware display, sending patterns skidding everywhere.

The man behind the counter bellowed and an alarm sounded as he hurled obscenities and threats at the men fighting in the showroom. She wanted to cover her ears and curl into a ball in the corner.

Sure way to die, that pesky know-it-all voice in her head said. Gaining her feet again, ignoring a spike of pain in her wrist, she skirted the men grappling for control of the knife and edged closer to the door.

"Oh, no you don't." A heavy, hairy arm caught her around the waist.

She twisted to find the massive man had come out of his cage. She squirmed against him, but his bulk seemed to absorb her efforts to escape. He was sweaty and cursing and there was blood soaking the hem of her shirt. Her shirt with a hole in it, she saw belatedly.

For some reason, that was the last straw. Not the blood, not the fighting men, but the ruined shirt. She didn't want to waste a dollar of her survival money on a replacement. Now that her face was on the pawn shop's security camera and police were on the way she had to move.

"Let me go!" He dragged her back, pinning her even more tightly to his flabby gut. Furious, she stomped on the top of his foot. He grunted but didn't release her.

She threw an elbow as close to his ribs as possible. Nothing seemed to faze him. They were almost to the cage and she didn't think she'd last long back there in his territory. She grabbed a display case and refused to let go. The strength of her grasp pulled her forward over his arm. He bent over to pry her fingers away and she threw her head back, connecting with his face. The resulting crack as her head broke his nose urged her on.

With a violent oath, he released her to cover his wounded face. She darted away, straight for the front door, barely registering that one of the men fighting was the redhead who'd been on her tail.

The police were racing down the block as she slipped outside. They yelled for her to stop, to freeze, but she kept on running and prayed for some kind of luck to go her way.

COLIN SAW his target dash away and cursed the timely arrival of the cops that prevented him from following her. His gut told him he'd have a hell of a time finding her again if he lost her now. She'd squeezed right through the crowd gathered outside gawking and hoping for an interesting fight. Since when did the Denver PD respond to calls in this neighborhood with such speed and enthusiasm? It wasn't uncommon for police to have a working understanding with pawn shops. A factor Summer probably hadn't known about when she'd walked in a few minutes ago.

He had to get out of here, fast, before her trail went cold. The responding officers would never let him waltz out of here with nothing but a thank you for saving a woman from a deadly assault. No, it would take too long to sort out the various statements of the man Colin had knocked out and the oversized worker holding his bleeding nose.

All of this ran through his head in a lightning-fast breakdown of possibilities. Colin bolted through the open door and into the cage, pulling the door shut and locking out the others. Heedless of the indignant protests and orders to halt chasing him, he ran through the back room and straight into the alley. The stench of rotting trash from the big metal bins almost drove him back inside.

He held his breath and pressed forward, his long stride carrying him down the block and around the corner. Losing her wasn't an acceptable outcome. Sure he wanted to protect his successful reputation within the agency. That had always been a motivator. Add in the knowledge that former SEAL Hank Patterson was watching and that motivation ratcheted higher still.

More than any of that was the woman herself. In the past twenty-four hours, he'd practically memorized her file and analyzed every additional snippet of information they dug up on her.

Summer Curley had proven more resourceful than he'd expected from a rather sheltered high school teacher from rural Montana.

He and Tyler had been searching nonstop and coming up empty. On a whim, Tyler had decided to see if he could spot the shooter at the diner or anyone tracking *her*. The kid was brilliant, Colin had to admit it. That tactic had been their breakthrough, the saving grace that led them to Denver. His assistant would blister his ears if Colin blew it and rendered all of that work useless.

With the would-be killer currently incapacitated back in the pawn shop, this was Colin's first advantage and his best opportunity to get Summer to a safe house. He continued running down the first block, dodging people and hoping she hadn't doubled back. At least here, there were enough security cameras for Tyler to tap into and if Colin got too far off the trail, his assistant would call.

At the next intersection, he swore. No sign of her and there were too many options between streets and businesses. Half-tempted to stand there and scream her name, he reached for his phone and called his assistant as he scanned the streets for any sign of her.

"North, north, north," Tyler said.

Colin was moving before he'd finished the second syllable.

"Drug store on your right," Tyler said. "She just went inside."

Colin ended the call and tucked the phone into his pocket. As much as he complained about too many cameras and an over-observed society, he was grateful for it now. And for his snarky assistant who could probably hack the NSA's hall monitors.

He wasn't subtle at all about looking for her, though he managed not to shout her name as he rushed along each aisle. He was running out of store to search when he saw a smear of blood on the grunge-gray linoleum floor that might once have been white. Colin's vision hazed red. That bastard with the knife had got her?

For the first time in a long time, he regretted working alone. In the past he would've given an order for someone to stay with her so he could go back and mete out some street justice.

Instead, he followed a trail of blood droplets from the initial smear through the first aid aisle and into the short hallway where the public restroom was located. He tested the handle. Locked. Pressing his ear to the door, he listened for any clue about who was inside, then he knocked.

"Almost done," a woman answered.

He'd never heard her voice, so he couldn't be sure, but all the pieces added up that this was the woman who needed his protection.

"Summer?" He jiggled the handle again. "Let me in. Let me help."

She didn't open the door, but she didn't yell at him or scream for security either.

He could break in with relative ease, but he propped a shoulder against the door frame to wait her out. "How bad is it?"

"Go away."

He cocked his head. It sounded as if she was pressed right up against the door. "That bad? I can help." He pitched his voice low so they wouldn't be overheard. "Hamilton sent me. I'm one of the good guys, I swear."

"Like a bad guy would admit such a thing."

In his experience, bad guys often telegraphed their unpleasant intentions. Of course, he'd been trained to recognize the signs. This wasn't about him or his training. "Hamilton hired me to protect you," he repeated. "My name is Colin. I work for the Guardian Agency. She wants me to bring you in, keep you safe."

The door handle moved the slightest bit and he fought the temptation to force his way in.

"Is there another way out of the bathroom?"

"No." The single word, full of defeat was accompanied by a thud against the door.

"So you're hoping I'll be hauled out of here for loitering?"

"Could that happen?"

"No." They were, however, still too close to the scuffle at the pawn shop. He wasn't the only person capable of following a blood trail. "If the cops notice your blood trail and follow it we're both screwed," he said. "Plus there's a hundred cameras in here. You need to get out of here, which means you need me."

"Or you're saying all that so I'll open the door for you to come in and kill me."

"The man hunting you wouldn't bother. He'd break in and take care of business."

Silence. "Look, the guy who cut you isn't feeling so hot right now and the cops will have a few questions for him. This is our chance." The store security guard strolled over, blocking the hallway from the rest of the store and giving him a hard glare. Great.

"Sweetheart, come on," he cajoled, in what he hoped came off as happy anticipation.

The man raised an eyebrow, one hand resting on the radio clipped to his belt. Likely a straight line to the police department.

Colin pointed at the door. "She's been queasy in

the mornings, y'know?" He crossed his fingers. "She had to go, so, *um*, we figured why not pee on a stick here?"

The guard's wary expression softened just a fraction. "Hurry it up."

"Come on, sweetheart," he said. "Let me see." Any second now someone else might tell the guard they hadn't purchased the test she wasn't using.

He was reaching for the door handle when it swung open. She lunged at him and he caught her hard against his chest. Not much to her, he thought, his body automatically calculating the shape and feel of hers.

Slender. His hand molded to the subtle curve of her waist. It took willpower not to follow that soft flare down to her hip. He pressed one hand along her delicate spine, trying to sell the embrace as a willing, happy thing on both sides. She felt like a bird in his hands, a creature he had no right to contain.

She looked up at him, at his hair. "You—"

He stepped her back into the bathroom and kicked the door closed. Setting her at arm's length, he looked her over head to toe. Her shirt was trashed, gaping open on one side and revealing a hastily applied bandage. He took in the bathroom in one fast glance. She'd lost a good bit of blood.

"Don't kill me," she pleaded, scooting out of his reach.

"If I wanted you dead, it would be done by now."

Her eyes, the darkest brown he'd ever seen, went wide, her straight eyebrows lifting toward her mussed hair. He had the ridiculous urge to comb her hair for her and wash the blood from her fingernails and the tears from her cheeks. The strange sensation rippled over his vision, hovering in the air between them. She was a mess, and hands-down the most beautiful woman he'd laid eyes on.

"Hamilton sent me," he said again. "I will protect you." He walked over and tucked the tattered shirt into the waistband of her jeans. He pulled her jacket closed and zipped it up to hide the wound and bloody shirt. "Do you think you can run?"

She nodded, letting him take her hand in his. "You've been following me," she whispered as he moved to the checkout counter by way of the family planning aisle. He grabbed a test and kept moving.

"We need to pay for one of these," he said sheepishly to the woman behind the checkout counter.

"I picked one up and used it already. Threw the box in the bathroom trash," she added. "Sorry."

The clerk, Tina according to her nametag, rolled her eyes. "It happens."

Noticing a rack of sunglasses, he picked up a pair and tried them on. "These too." He handed them over to be scanned. The future is bright."

"All right." She looked from Colin to Summer and back again. "At least you two seem happy about the results."

He pulled Summer close and dropped a kiss on her head as he accepted his change. "We're thrilled."

Mostly he was thrilled they hadn't been cornered yet. He was overjoyed that she'd played along so well. Down the block, lights from two police cars flashed and crime scene tape was going up. He walked casually in the opposite direction, his arm slung over her shoulders.

"Easy," he coached in her ear. "We're a couple now. They're looking for a woman alone and injured."

"*Mm-hm.*"

"As soon as we're off the street, you can call Hamilton and verify my story if it helps."

She didn't respond and her footsteps were sluggish. She leaned heavily into his side. She was worse off than he'd thought. Damn. They needed to keep moving at a much better clip.

A white sedan pulled up beside them and the passenger window rolled down. "Are you Mr. Hazard?"

"Who's asking?" Colin catalogued every detail of the driver's face.

"A guy named Tyler said you needed a ride and sent me over."

"Great." Colin made a mental note to recommend a bonus for Tyler as he settled Summer into the back seat of the compact car. "Did he tell you my destination too?"

"Actually, yes." He named a high-end hotel chain near the airport as he merged with the traffic on the street. They were out of the seedy neighborhood and immediate danger within a few minutes.

Colin let his head fall back as the glitter of the city flowed by the windows. One day, he was going to meet Tyler and give the man a hug. He didn't care if it went against any professional code or crossed personal boundaries. This instance alone merited a serious demonstration of gratitude.

CHAPTER 3

SUMMER FELT as if her brain had been swaddled in cotton. Everything was soft and fuzzy around the edges. She didn't think she'd lost enough blood to be this woozy, but she couldn't seem to pull anything into focus long enough to figure out what happened.

The fabric under her hands was silky smooth and cool. The air smelled fresh and clean enough to breathe deeply. Doing so made her wince as pain pinched her side.

"Take it easy."

The gentle, mellow tone cut a wedge through the fog. That voice didn't fit anything in her memory. A blast of fear cleared her mind and she opened her eyes, blinking rapidly. Slowly her gaze focused on the redheaded man who'd been following her. He was sitting in a chair beside the bed, watching her with those enigmatic hazel eyes. The green was more pronounced at the moment, reminding her of that kaleidoscope of late summer color in the trees around the house where she grew up.

He had an interesting face to go with those changeable eyes. She liked the straight nose dusted with faint freckles and the scruffy whiskers shot with gold shading his strong jawline. His mouth seemed ready to flash into a smirk or an outright grin at any moment. She had the oddest thought that his smile would send her heart into palpitations.

He'd been there in the pawn shop and after. Providing help or just nudging her into his trap? His presence didn't clarify a thing about her situation, though she figured he must be the good guy he'd claimed to be since she wasn't in police custody or dead.

"Have you been watching me sleep?" Her opinion of him dipped back toward possibly-dangerous creep.

"Not exactly." Those lips remained stoic. "I've made sure you're safe and comfortable."

"Where am I? Who are you, really?" She twisted her wrists, flexed her hands and feet, making sure she hadn't been restrained. Ignoring the domino effect of prickling twinges just under her rib cage to another sharp, outright pain low on her side, she worked herself upright. She couldn't have a conversation with this man while lying on her back.

"Easy," he repeated. "You passed out on the drive

here." He moved closer and adjusted the pillows behind her back. "You're in a hotel suite and I'm Colin Hazard, your bodyguard for the foreseeable future."

"What if I don't want to be in a hotel suite under your protection?" she challenged. "Can I leave?"

His eyes, so warm and kind and focused on her turned cool and his gaze shifted to the window across the room. "I don't recommend you going anywhere just yet, but technically you *can* go." Before she could move he added, "Should you leave, be aware that I will follow you."

She threw back the sheet and thin blanket, discovering too late she was wearing only her bra and panties. And a stark white bandage on her side. She yanked the covers back, clutching the fabric under her chin. "You...you stripped me?"

"Only as a professional courtesy," he deadpanned. "There's no additional charge."

There was a glimmer in his eyes. Appreciation? Interest? Why did that glimmer light a spark under her skin? She should be outraged, she was, and yet an edgy giggle bubbled out of her. So much for crafting a more dignified and appropriate response.

She had a weakness for lingerie and despite her modest salary, she religiously scrimped and saved to buy pretty pieces no one else ever saw. Under the sheet, she ran her fingers along the edge of the bandage he'd applied. That was the source of her earlier pain. Why didn't she have any memory of him taking care of her? It was a crime in itself that a sexy man undressed her, treated a wound, tucked her into bed and yet she couldn't recall a single moment.

"Did you drug me or something?"

"No." His ginger eyebrows snapped down, clearly offended. "I didn't see any signs that you're an addict."

"Of course I'm not. I just don't understand blacking out the way I did."

"Adrenaline, blood loss, shock. It adds up. If it helps, you flitted in and out there for a while." He plucked a bottle of water from the nightstand and handed it to her. "Here. You need fluids."

She appreciated that he let her open the bottle, proving it was sealed to start with. The cool liquid soothed her throat, cooled the heat of embarrassment flooding her system. "Thank you for helping me," she said after she'd downed half the bottle.

"Doing my job." He sat back in the chair near the bed.

"Have you been here—right here—the whole time?"

"Give or take." He shrugged. "It's not as creepy as it sounds. Just the way it works. I get an order to protect a person and I go out and do that. People survive and the good guys win."

He'd loaded plenty of attitude in those simple statements, but she sensed that his success rate was important to him. She appreciated the value of stats. "You're a professional bodyguard."

"One of the best," he said in that same just-the-facts tone. "Would you like to call Hamilton and verify my role here?"

She should definitely call and verify. She would do it too, just as soon as the idea of speaking with the U.S. Attorney's office didn't make her queasy. The upcoming trial had been the focal point of her entire world for months. She'd distracted herself with an update to her class curriculum, including drafting a presentation for an educator's conference she hoped to attend next year. With nothing else occupying her time, the project had been finished too quickly and didn't do much to ease the deeply buried guilt and stress over her sister's ordeal.

She'd immersed herself in dozens of books on various topics, from teaching to self-help. Although it had been a prickly process on the best of days, she drafted numerous letters to both her father and her sister asking for forgiveness, sharing her hope of reconciliation. The letters weren't meant to be delivered, only to give her an emotional outlet. The exercise hadn't made a dent in her persistent nightmares about the day Autumn had been kidnapped and what her sister must have endured during her years under the mob's control.

Autumn's survival and escape was nothing short of a miracle, but Summer's dream of a reunion had been dashed by the legal system. Her sister couldn't come home because the people behind the operation wanted her dead and the prosecutors needed her alive to testify against them.

"Do you know anything about my sister's situation? Last I heard she was in protective custody too. If they found me…" She couldn't bring herself to finish the sentence. And if the gangs found her sister again, they'd never let her live.

Colin propped one booted ankle on his knee, his gaze on the laces. "According to my assistant, three witness locations were compromised. My agency has been called in to protect all three of you."

That didn't help much since she had no idea how many witnesses Hamilton had chosen to protect. "Was… Was my sister's location compromised?" The query scalded her throat.

"Yes," he replied. "That's my understanding. Along with the woman who helped her escape."

Summer wanted to curl up into a ball and black out again. She wanted to shut off the world, to find a place where her memory of Autumn being dragged away into unspeakable horrors couldn't reach her.

"You're safe," Colin said. "As is the woman who owned the café where Autumn initially escaped her captors."

She pinched the blanket into small fans between her fingers, dreading the rest of his report.

"My assistant tells me your sister hasn't been found yet. Everyone is assuming that's good news."

She gawked at him. "You're kidding."

"I'm not. The gang at the head of this operation would have made an example of her if they'd found her. They wouldn't hide her death, they'd advertise it as a cautionary tale."

That was true. As a high school teacher on the reservation, she'd heard the rumors and seen some of the results at the lower end of the gang system. The gangs at the top of the Native Mob ladder were known for even more intense ruthlessness. Snitches and traitors weren't tolerated.

"Without Autumn the men who did this to her will walk," she murmured. Making a waste of all of the time and resources that kept her and the others protected before the trial. Her stomach twisted and she was glad all she'd had was the water.

"I wouldn't give up on the justice system quite so fast," he said. "We found you and the other woman. We'll find your sister before they do."

She wasn't sure how much faith in the justice system she had left. Whether or not the men paid for their crimes, her family was in ruins. One sister missing, the other all but banished for letting it happen. Not that Summer could have done anything to prevent those men from hauling her sister away. None of that changed the present.

"How long have I been out?"

"Are you hungry?"

Their questions collided and they both stopped talking. She couldn't help but smile when he did, even though the man, the situation, rattled her on several levels.

"You're safe," he said again, as if eventually she'd believe it. "I can order some food while you talk to Hamilton," he offered. "You might feel better once she verifies that my only role here is to help you."

"I'm not sure if I should call," she said. "I mean, yes it is common sense to verify your story, but…" Her thoughts were a jumble of what ifs and worst case scenarios. "Do you know how they found the witnesses in the first place?"

He frowned, that charming smile gone. "No."

"You've let them know I'm off the street, under your protection?" When he nodded, she made her decision to trust him. He could've killed her or turned her over a dozen times by now. She'd been at his mercy for a few hours. And he just didn't give off the vibe that he was about to flip loyalties on her.

That didn't mean he wasn't dangerous. He just wasn't dangerous to her the way the criminals were dangerous. No, Colin was dangerous like a box of decadent chocolates or an excellent red wine. Tempting her to indulge in ways that wouldn't end well in the long term.

"Is that sunrise or sunset out there?" From her vantage point, she could only see daylight on the other side of the window and she had no intention of parading around in her underwear to check the view.

"It's late afternoon. You've only been out a couple of hours." He stretched out his legs. "You made good time getting from Helena to Denver."

For all the good it had done. "And I was found and stabbed in record time as well." She needed to up her game if she was going to avoid trouble once the trial was over. Maybe Colin could give her some advice.

"I'm guessing I spooked you," he said, staring at the floor. "For what it's worth, you didn't show any sign that you'd noticed me."

"Is that a good thing?"

He lifted his gaze and when his eyes met hers, she felt it as distinctly as a touch. "Can be, depending on the job."

"Oh."

She really should *not* be fascinated by the gold flecks glinting in the rough whiskers outlining his jaw. And she had no business trying to sort out exactly what turned his eyes more green than brown. Hazel was enough information between client and bodyguard.

"Thanks for taking care of me."

"I admit I worried that the knife had been treated with some kind of drug that caused you to faint," he said, "But you haven't shown more adverse reactions since. Drink up." He gestured for her to finish off the water. "Looks like the blood loss was just the last jolt your body could tolerate. Adrenaline takes a toll."

"I've heard as much."

"Better for you to eat well and rest through tonight." He planted his hands on his knees, then stood up. "I'll get the room service menu."

Room service was too pricey. She didn't have the cash to cover that kind of splurge. She didn't even know how the money for this kind of thing worked. Embarrassed all over again, she scooted to the edge of the bed. "Please don't. I'll dress and we can go somewhere. Fast food sounds good actually."

He stared at her, his gaze so intense she was sure he saw past skin and muscle and bone straight to the truth and doubts and recriminations staining her very soul. "You aren't ready to go out," he said at last.

"I can be," she insisted. The sheet twisted around her legs and she struggled. "Just give me a few minutes."

To her further humiliation, he walked over and freed her, his movements firm and confident. Her mind flashed back to the way his hands had felt on her in that drug store restroom. Strong and steady. Stabilizing. She'd surged through the door and tried to fight him and he'd effortlessly subdued her. Yet he hadn't pushed his obvious advantage. He hadn't hurt her or made her feel less.

She didn't know what to do with that.

"You need to rest for as long as possible. Worry and pushing too hard, starving yourself won't help."

"Why are you being nice to me?" she demanded.

"You're the client," he replied. "My agency prefers for me to be courteous."

"So all of this—" she flung out her hand to encompass the luxurious room, "is on the U.S. Attorney's tab?"

"As I said before, there's no charge to you for any of the upgrades." His eyebrows bobbed up and down in an overstated comical manner. "Seems to me you enjoy nice things."

Too late, she remembered she was standing there in her high-end, sexy underwear. "Occasionally, yes." What was the point of modesty now, if he'd seen it all as he'd taken care of her? Some bikinis were skimpier that what she wore, so she brazened it out, not bothering with the sheet again. Clearly he was right and she was in no condition to go anywhere.

"Summer, is it okay if I call you that?"

"You have been," she snapped, immediately feeling contrite. "Yes, it's okay," she managed.

"Good. And you'll call me Colin." He looked as if he might touch her and then tucked his hands into the pockets of what she recognized as pricey jeans. "We're almost friends already. No one is going to send you a bill when this is over. All you have to do is rest and let me protect you until you can testify."

She nodded, not trusting her voice.

"So you'll eat, you'll rest, and then we'll figure out what to do next."

Without a reliable voice she couldn't argue. Nodding, she took another step toward the bathroom. What was it about the man that made her want to trust him so quickly? Maybe it was the freckles. There was something innocent about freckles in general. And Colin was different from the people she usually saw in her day to day life. She liked the warmth in his eyes and the sly tilt to his mouth.

That mouth kicked up at one corner and bloomed into a grin. He folded his arms over his chest, waiting for her to do or say something. The banked heat in his eyes convinced her he enjoyed the view, but he wasn't lecherous about it. She was practically ogling him as well. Thank goodness her deeper skin tone made high intensity blushes less obvious.

"What are you hungry for?" he asked before she could close the door.

"I'll eat anything at this point," she admitted.

"Fine." His brows snapped together. "Don't get that bandage wet."

"I'll be careful." At last she was alone again, away from the enticing gaze of the man who'd rescued her. She looked around in awe. The bathroom finishes matched the well-appointed details of the bedroom. An expansive marble counter, a glass shower with multiple sprayers, and towels so thick and fluffy she might get swallowed up whole.

She felt a surge of guilt about hiding in such an indulgent place when she had no idea about her sister's whereabouts or circumstance. What was one more layer heaped on top of the guilt she'd been carrying since Autumn was kidnapped?

Resigned, she soaked a washcloth in warm water at the sink before pressing it to her face. It was high time she found the logical, practical woman she'd always been. She had to be smart about getting through this botched trial if she had any chance of rebuilding her family.

COLIN BRIEFLY CONSIDERED GOING out for a bucket of ice. To dump over his head. A cold shower wouldn't be enough. Nothing would ever erase the vision of Summer's glorious body from his mind. All that golden skin highlighted by the sunlight from the window and her subtle curves cradled in all the right places by black satin would fuel his fantasies for years to come.

His palms tingled in anticipation of cupping the soft weight of her breasts.

She was a client. How many times had he told her she was safe with him? He couldn't let lust blur that line. This case was too important. Hell, even if the case had been petty theft, a woman's life vastly outweighed this hunger.

Disgusted with himself, he read the full description of each item on the room service menu. He was ravenous, a typical state for him, and she needed to get her strength back. Too bad Tyler's research hadn't uncovered her favorite foods yet. He called in an order, covering all his bases from salad to burgers.

As soon as the task was done, his mind whipped right back to the beautiful sway of her hips as she'd walked into the bathroom.

Of course he'd noticed her body when he'd undressed her, but that had been more clinical, his mind locked into the context of treating her wound and praying the blade hadn't been dipped in poison. The knife hadn't pierced anything vital, much to his relief. It was the way it had sliced through her skin that led to the excessive bleeding. Using his first aid kit, he'd stitched her up, applied antibiotic ointment and covered the wound. At the time, he'd been relieved she'd been out of it.

Then he'd kept watch, not for intruders, but for any sign of further decline. Her sudden collapse in the car had worried him more than he would ever admit to her or to Tyler. When she'd passed out his mind had dragged him back, unwillingly, into that dank cave of hopelessness. Those frailties were supposed to be well behind him. He wasn't an idiot. He was fully aware that the Guardian Agency kept a close eye on him because of his past. But he was as determined as they were that what happened overseas wouldn't interfere with his new career.

"Colin?"

Her voice carried from the bedroom. "Where are my clothes?"

When he turned, she was in the doorway, her lithe body swallowed by the stark white fluff of the hotel robe. It required serious effort to keep his eyes on her face when he wanted to take her all in, inch by delectable inch.

"I sent your jeans and jacket to be cleaned," he said. "The shirt was a lost cause."

Her lips thinned as she watched him, wary. With good reason, since his body was prodding him to flirt with her until she was tucked back into bed and he was stretched out beside her. Over her. That stray thought was all it took. He was hard and ready for her and not even her status as a client, as a woman under his *protection* quelled that fresh blast of lust.

"I can't go around without a shirt," she muttered.

She could, according to his overactive and inappropriate imagination. "We'll take care of the clothing after you eat." He hated the way her eyes clouded at his brusque tone. "Food should be here shortly."

She padded closer, pausing to run her hands over the upholstered couch. Why could he feel that touch in his shoulders? "Do all bodyguards go overboard like this?"

He couldn't make sense of the question, what with most of his blood rushing south of his belt. "Pardon me?"

"This posh suite, room service." She flicked one long-fingered hand at him. "You." Her chest rose and fell on a sharp breath. "Shouldn't we be at some budget motel?"

"I keep telling you you're not paying a dime," he assured her. "The bills go to Hamilton."

"And the taxpayers," she murmured.

What was her issue with money? "True. Although I got the impression that Hamilton and my agency have some kind of understanding. Taxpayers pay for prisoners too," he said trying to ease these apparent concerns she had about being a burden. "Protecting witnesses should be a better experience than we give criminals."

"I suppose you're right."

He was definitely right on that, if nothing else. "If it helps, I chose this place because security is better than it would be at some seedy motel. The surveillance cameras work, there's an actual team, and that means one more layer of protection for you."

"Oh." The lines of tension around her face faded and her slow smile was almost shy as she caressed the fabric of the robe. "I'll try to enjoy it then."

"Do that," he said through clenched teeth. He wanted to enjoy her, to let her stroke him the way she was fondling the robe. "Wasn't the safe house nice?"

"It was," she said quickly. "We were in an upper-middle class house in the heart of suburbia," she said, crossing to the big window that allowed light to fill the common area of the suite. "A lovely neighborhood I couldn't enjoy except through the windows."

"You enjoy nature?"

She nodded without turning. "I grew up on a farm on the Crow Reservation. Nature was about the only entertainment we had, but I loved it."

The farm had been in her file, of course, but bare facts rarely told the whole story. He and Summer were wildly different, from their backgrounds and upbringing to their career choices. She taught high school math in a rural school. He was a former soldier, a former prisoner of war, and a brand new bodyguard trying to out-work the nightmares haunting him.

Nothing about her should entice him, even before he factored in her status as the client. He was better than this, had endured violent torture tactics with more self-control than he was displaying right now.

"What happened to the farm?" Had it been sold? No one had figured out why she'd come to Denver when the background research indicated her strongest ties were to home and friends closer to the reservation.

"You'd have to ask my dad," she replied quietly.

"He hasn't allowed me to step foot on the property since Autumn was taken."

He perched on the arm of the couch, watching her. "You're serious."

When she turned around, the sadness stamped on her face made her look more vulnerable than when he'd been dealing with her wound. Despite his fraught relationship with his parents they'd never banned him from the family estate. He just never wanted to go back to the perfectly manicured lawns, the fussy, exquisite rooms and the overstuffed expectations of what he should do with his life.

"I'm the oldest," she said. "He believes I should have done more to protect her." She wrapped her arms tight around her middle. "He isn't wrong."

While she'd slept, he'd read the case file again. He'd gone over and over her statement she'd given to police when her sister was kidnapped. He was looking at her now, imagining the two burly men who'd hauled her sister away. "What could you have done? Her kidnappers would've destroyed you," he said. An ugly thought coiled in his belly. "Or taken you along."

He paced away from her, beyond uncomfortable with the sudden fury surging through his system. He had no claim on her, hell they'd just met. This over-the-top possessiveness must be some new outlet for the anger and grief his shrink claimed he kept bottled up.

It was hardly a soothing or calming thought, but nothing else made sense under these circumstances. He was saved from further self-assessment by the knock at the door.

He pressed a finger to his lips and signaled for her to hide in the bedroom. The odds were low that they'd been found by the people hunting her, but he wasn't taking any chances until she was stronger. Peering through the peep hole, he saw a fresh-faced kid in a hotel uniform, fingers tapping on the edge of the room service cart. Not the guy he'd tangled with in the pawn shop.

The kid knocked again and Colin waited one more second before opening the door.

"Hello, sir." The kid beamed. "Shall I set this out for you?"

Colin stepped back, allowing him to come in with the cart. "Just leave it at the table."

"Oh, but I can—"

The kid's voice faded when he caught sight of Colin's expression. Or more likely the twenty dollar bill between his fingers.

The kid stepped closer and Colin held the money tightly. "Anyone ask about this order?"

"No, sir."

"Anyone new in the kitchen today?"

"No, sir." The kid frowned a little, his gaze sliding to the door. He was obviously torn between making an escape and hanging in for the hefty tip.

"Last question," Colin said. "Did anyone ride up on the elevator with you?"

"No, sir."

"Great." He pushed the money into the kid's palm. "Thanks for everything. Have a great night."

"Yes, sir. You too."

He was out of the suite as if he'd been shot from a cannon. Colin walked over and rapped on Summer's door. "All clear."

She came into view, her robe gapping open. She'd taken the belt and wrapped the ends around each of her hands with enough length to strangle someone.

"Resourceful. I like it." He admired the ingenuity even as that sliver of a view stirred him up again. The bed behind her was too damn close. Walking toward the table was like slogging through thick mud. "Come get something to eat."

By the time she reached the table, she was completely covered again. He tried not to regret it. The lack of a view was safer for both of them. "I didn't see anything in your file about food allergies." Uncovering the various plates, he urged more water on her. "What looks good to start?"

Her stomach rumbled loudly and they both chuckled. "The salad, please."

He placed the big bowl in front of her and watched her drizzle the dressing over the bed of mixed greens, grilled chicken, fresh berries and chopped pecans. "It's weird that you know so much about me." Taking her first bite, she closed her eyes and sighed.

He didn't know half of what he wanted to know. Wrenching his gaze from her blissful expression, he dragged his thoughts back to the case and took a mammoth bite of a fully loaded cheeseburger. Not the healthiest choice, but he figured he deserved it after the fight and chasing her down.

He had questions about her previous security detail, about her escape from Helena, and her decision to hide in Denver. But he could wait until she fueled up. He'd learned the hard way that the wrong topic of conversation could undo all the benefits of a good meal.

"You seem extremely at ease with all of this. Does this happen often?" she queried, snagging a cookie from the tray.

"Each case is different," he said. "Variety is one of the things I enjoy about my work. Hotels and room service aren't always involved," he said. He caught her staring at him while she pressed a napkin to her lips. Was she laughing at him? "What's so funny?"

"I just can't see you in a kitchen any more than I can see you slumming around in a cheap motel. That's what stood out on the street earlier. You were too fancy for the neighborhood."

He wasn't about to apologize for that. Once he'd returned to the States he'd vowed never to settle for less than the best. He'd earned it. "I like nice things."

She smiled. "An understatement. You like top of the line things," she said. "The sunglasses you bought at the drug store are probably the closest you've come to slumming in your life."

"Not true." Rattled by her assessment, he stood up and walked away from the table. Experience colored everyone's opinions and decisions. It sounded like she'd had a near-poverty start in life, he hadn't. He'd been a prisoner, she'd only been subject to protective custody. Bottom line, she didn't know him and she didn't need to. They'd go their separate ways as soon as she testified in Hamilton's case.

"I'm confident this suite is a vast improvement over wherever you planned to stay." He couldn't quell the defensive tone.

Her chin came up. "I was making my cash stretch until I came up with a plan."

"A smart move. Now I can help you implement a better plan. You can recuperate in a clean and secure environment. All your needs can be met right here until you're ready to head back to Montana. You said you were going to try and enjoy it," he reminded her.

She glared at him and he wondered what the hell he'd done wrong. Not everyone was delighted to have a bodyguard, but this bickering was new to him. He had to try and get them to a place where they could communicate. "I'm not criticizing you." He dug his fingers into the tight muscles at the back of his neck. "If you hadn't been nicked I might still be out there searching for you."

"You mean it?" She perked up at the compliment and he had to smother a smile.

"Never saw much sense in saying things I don't mean."

She chose another cookie. "How long do you think we'll stay?"

He was half-afraid to tell her. "Two days, maybe three?"

She eyed the cookie. "Two or three days of eating like this and my jeans won't fit." She took another bite and gave a little hum of appreciation. "But I will enjoy it."

The sparkle in her dark eyes made him chuckle. "I'm glad to hear it."

"I haven't meant to sound so ungrateful." She licked the crumbs from her fingertips. "It's just bewildering. Protective custody was a bizarre experience. Of course I knew there was a world of nicer things outside our farm. I never envied any of it, but I confess I do feel unsettled in places that are so far out of my purview."

"You sound like a woman scrambling for control," he said gently. He wasn't sure where the gentleness was coming from, but he was grateful to tap into the unexpected reserve. "I'm not here to challenge that, but protect it. It's my job to see that your needs are met."

"Needs are one thing." She spread her arms to encompass the room, the robe gapping enough to give him another peek of the satin bra. "This is above and beyond." She covered her face with her hands. "I'm sorry," she said, her voice muffled. "I'm being an idiot. Of course I'm thankful for the food, the care, the safety."

He'd seen worse reactions, occasionally in the mirror. "Don't sweat it. This sort of thing is hard on everyone."

"The fantasy or the reality?" She peeked up at him, those dark eyes glittering with emotions.

He couldn't handle that look, those words, when he was so short on sleep himself. He walked over to the coffee machine and set a cup to brew. "I'm not sure I'm following." Other than his ill-timed obsession with her body, he couldn't figure out what qualified as fantasy on her side.

"I'm a numbers girl," she said. "I can't stop doing the math, even when I know it's not my money directly on the line. A suite like this is a luxury I've only read about. Even on someone else's dime it makes my skin crawl. Probably the same way my dingy room would've made your skin crawl."

"You wouldn't have been safe or happy in a dingy room tonight. No one could be." She shrugged, but didn't argue the point. "I gave you my reasons. The upscale security here gives me a chance to rest too. No one can go twenty-four-seven indefinitely and stay sharp." He raised his coffee cup in a mock salute.

"My passing out proves that point, I guess." She pulled her knees to her chest, her hands curled around her ankles. "I'm in over my head whether we're in a pawn shop or a fancy hotel. Marie told me to run, to hide. Not to trust anyone but her." She looked up at him. "But I trust you."

"Thanks for that." He came back to the table and picked up a chocolate chunk cookie. "You've been through an ordeal, Summer. I can hope the worst is behind you, but there are no guarantees. At least with me around, you aren't in it alone anymore."

His cell phone rang and he managed to smother the curse before it got past his lips. "This is my assistant," he explained. "Stay and listen," he suggested when she stood up.

She sat back down, her eyes wide.

"Hey, Tyler, you're on speaker." He set the phone on the table between them.

"Hi," Tyler replied. He cleared his throat. "Hello, Ms. Curley."

"Hello." She braced her forearms on the table.

Tyler launched into his report, covering the basics about progress on the police investigation into the fight at the pawn shop. Colin listened while watching Summer's reactions.

"Bottom line, I'm confident the police will eventually track you to the hotel," Tyler finished.

"Cameras are everywhere these days," Summer murmured.

Sad but true. "No way to divert them?" Colin asked. "Should we get ahead of this and go give the police our statement?"

"Normally, I'd say yes." Tyler gave a heavy sigh. "In this case, it smells like a trap."

"Seriously?" He couldn't believe what he was hearing. "What stake does the Denver PD possibly have in this case?"

"None. It's more about who's *watching* the Denver PD stations," Tyler said. "The man who attacked Summer in the pawn shop escaped police custody."

Colin swore and slammed his fist down on the table. "Way to bury the lead," he barked. "Someone must have taken a bribe. No one is that incompetent."

"I don't think that's it," Tyler said. "No one had any idea the Native Mob has this kind of reach. Denver PD had the guy handcuffed in the back of a patrol car. The car was pinched a block from the station. Nothing the officers could do. I'm surprised they weren't killed."

Summer gasped, her gorgeous, sunlit skin going pale.

"The woman who helped Autumn escape is out of danger," Tyler continued. "The trial appears to be going forward on the revised schedule. Ms. Curley will need to be back in Helena soon. I'll let you know when we have a hard date."

"And Autumn?" Colin asked the question for Summer.

"No one has found her yet. All I can tell you is we're not the only ones looking."

She dropped her head to her hands, massaging her temples. He wanted to soothe her, to take every last unpleasantness and cast it out of her life.

He shook it off. The job—keeping a client safe—was a simple task on the surface. The logistics of that task often had to be adjusted mid-stride and this case was sure to keep him on his toes. Thinking on his feet was one of his top skills and his years with the Army had only made those skills stronger. "Recommendations?" he asked Tyler.

For a moment the only sound was the soft rapid-fire tapping of Tyler's keyboard. "Hold your ground. You aren't registered in your name and although your face is clear on the camera, hers isn't."

"But how many semi-conscious women could you have possibly hauled up here?" Summer muttered.

"I hear ya," Tyler said with a short laugh. "The lack of facial recognition will buy you some more time, even if they follow the car straight to the hotel portico."

"Right up until we step out of this room."

"Pretty much," Tyler agreed. "The mob looks disorganized and disjointed on paper. Obviously, they have more going on than anyone thought having breached witness protection records and sent in teams to, um, to…"

"We get it," Colin said. A professional hitman was on Summer's trail and he had a surprising amount of help. "Stay in touch and we'll do the same."

He ended the call quickly, his gaze locked with Summer's. "I can handle this. You have to trust me."

"My sister's out there alone."

It took him a second to switch gears. That wasn't what he expected from her. "You don't know that."

Summer stood up, wrapping her arms around her midsection. "I do. She's out there all by herself and here I sit in the lap of luxury, absolutely no help to her at all." Pain twisted her features and she scurried into the bedroom and slammed the door.

At last he started to see the bigger picture. She was dealing with more than her fair share of survivor guilt. Colin stared at that closed door for a long time, wondering how to help her through this impossible crisis. When he'd been in the Army, he'd been trained to give people what they expected, what they needed to hear.

Somehow he wanted to give Summer more than that. He wanted to give her some genuine promise that things would work out. Doing so would be a huge mistake. He *would* keep her safe, but that didn't seem to be enough to ease a deeper pain.

CHAPTER 4

Summer flopped down on the bed and buried her face in the pillow, afraid if she started to cry in earnest she'd never stop. She struggled to reconcile her past and present failings, searching for a way to make up for those mistakes. Except going back was impossible and there was no making up for her errors, no way to change what her sister had endured.

It was little comfort that Colin was right about her needing time to recover, although doing so here, in such a posh suite, only added another thick layer of guilt. Unless Autumn had forgotten herself during the two years since she'd been kidnapped, she would have wisely run away from any and all people. Summer had simply tossed herself from the frying pan into the fire. Her sister was the courageous and independent one, Summer was the idealistic fool who'd cut herself off from her roots. Or so said her father.

She rolled to her back, wincing as the movement tugged at the stitches. For a bodyguard, Colin made an excellent nurse. She peeked under the bandage and marveled at the neat row of stitches. It probably wouldn't leave much of a scar.

What kind of scars would Autumn have? Would her sister even speak to her again?

Summer fell asleep on those unanswered questions and woke up hours later to the soft light of dawn at the window. She immediately turned to the bedside chair and found it empty. Colin must have decided she wasn't so fragile after all. Why did his absence disappoint her?

Rolling out of bed she padded toward the bathroom, noticing a rolling suitcase near the closet that hadn't been there last night. Her jacket was on a hanger. In the bathroom, she found her jeans folded on the counter, along with two new tees, one long sleeve shirt, socks, and undergarments in the right sizes. She didn't want to know how he'd figured that out.

One of them had been busy overnight.

When she'd freshened up and dressed in the clean clothes, she followed the scent of coffee toward the suite's kitchenette. She stopped short at the sight of Colin sitting at the counter. Wearing only jeans, his torso and feet were bare. He wasn't bulked up like bodyguards in the movies, but no one would question his fitness. The man had a presence that made her pulse race. He shifted and she noticed the scars crisscrossing his back along with a jagged scar that started near his ribs and disappeared beneath his jeans.

What on earth had he been through? She swallowed back the question. It wasn't her business and he was concentrating on his cell phone. When he looked up those hazel eyes snared her. She felt utterly singed by the blast of heat in his gaze.

"Good morning," she managed.

"Yeah." He dragged one hand across his chest and his eyes went wide. He darted away to his room, the moment broken. When he returned, he wore a T-shirt with a logo for a video game a few of her students played online. "Morning," he said, smiling this time.

As if that would make it any easier for her to have a coherent thought.

"Coffee?" he offered.

She nodded. He was still closer to the coffeemaker. She forced herself to move closer to the counter. "I guess we're both up early."

"Feeling better?" he asked. "I see you found the clothes."

"Thanks for that," she said. Her skin went warm knowing she was wearing items he'd chosen. For her. "Have you had any rest?"

He placed the full mug of piping hot coffee on the counter for her. "Enough," he replied. "I was just reading through the update from Tyler. Now, there's a guy who doesn't slow down."

She sipped her coffee and waited for him to fill her in.

"He'd like us to stay here through tomorrow. In the morning we can start back to Helena. Hamilton is lobbying for a new court date, sooner rather than later. Her theory is if they can get this through a trial, there won't be any reason for the mob to hunt down the witnesses."

One more day in this beautifully appointed cage shouldn't be a hardship. She'd enjoy it a whole lot more if she knew her sister was all right. "You do realize revenge is the mob's stock in trade?"

He shrugged and picked up his coffee. "I got the impression she'll be diverting their focus from you and the others for a long time."

That would be nice. He hadn't mentioned her sister, so she assumed the 'missing' status remained the same. "Do you think the case has any chance without Autumn?"

"They have her deposition," Colin replied. "If push comes to shove, they'll work up a video for the jury." He pulled out the stool next to her and sat down.

She gave a little start, so lost in her worries over Autumn she hadn't heard him walk up behind her.

"Sorry." He adjusted the stool to give her more

space.

"Don't apologize." This close, she noticed the warm, masculine scent of his skin. The man was as unnerving as the suite. He'd ordered clothing for her, a suitcase, and personal items as well. She wasn't sure how he got it done. Or how she'd repay him. The expenses were covered, but she still felt indebted. She knew even if she offered the cash she had, he wouldn't take it.

Summer had been raised to believe circumstance was never a valid excuse to take a hand out. Her father constantly hammered home the message that people should strive to contribute to their community. It was a great theory until a crisis occurred. Every hour she spent with Colin, her body healed while her pride was more deeply bruised. Assuming he got her through this, she would find a way to give him something in return.

"I'm just antsy. This is a superb safe house, but—"

"You want your freedom," he finished for her.

"Yes!" She tucked a loose strand of hair behind her ear. "I can't believe you aren't feeling trapped."

"The view is worth it."

She turned to find him staring at her rather than the mountains outside the window. "Are you flirting with me?"

He grinned. "Could be," he admitted. "If a little flirting takes your mind off the whole mess then it becomes a requirement of my job."

"That's really flawed logic." She couldn't suppress a smile. This was a side of him she hadn't seen yet. One she could get used to in a hurry. "And it sounds complicated."

"Actually, I'm pretty simple."

She snorted. "Your actions prove you have layers."

"Want me to take them off?" He bobbed those ginger eyebrows again.

The cheesy move made her laugh. "Stop it." His hazel eyes hinted at loads of secrets under the light-hearted banter. She wasn't sure what to do with a man who could change from stern to charming and back again in the blink of an eye. His razor-sharp mind sorted through information swiftly and accurately. To her dismay, she found that as irresistibly attractive as his lean build and confident swagger.

It had to be a product of being so long by herself, far from her routine and watched over by strangers. Only Marie had bothered to really make a connection and now she was gone. She and Colin might be in a luxury hotel, but they were basically living out the hypothetical deserted island situation. He was the last man in her world and she wanted him. More with every conversation. Despite his caring and his heated looks and his attempts to put her at ease she knew better than to believe he truly wanted her the same way.

"How can I make this more tolerable?" he asked.

She slid off the stool and carried her coffee over

to the sitting area. "You've done more than enough. I'm fine," she assured him, dropping into a corner of the couch. The sun was up now and it looked like Denver was due for a gorgeous, clear day.

She popped up again, too restless to stay put. "Just anxious. About the case and my sister's safety." Pacing the width of the room, she counted her steps. There were always so many counters running in her head. One tracking her footsteps and another counting the days and hours since she'd last seen her sister. Usually those moving numbers calmed her, today they were no match for the situation.

"Is there anything we can do to find my sister?"

"Our agency—"

She cut him off with an impatient wave. "I'm sure you're all quite capable at the Guardian Agency." Her gaze drifted over his body and she turned on her heel to break the spell she so willingly fell into. "But maybe there's something I can add that would help. She's my little sister. I feel responsible."

"I understand that."

Behind her, his voice was so serious, it drew her in despite her best intentions. The proverbial moth to flame. The secrets swirling in his gaze were closer to the surface again. She wanted to hear his story even as she worried that in doing so she'd only become more attached to the unreachable fantasy of him.

"My dad blames me," she blurted.

"You mentioned that."

Had she? "If I could help find her, things might improve." He might actually forgive her. "He hasn't spoken to me since she went missing. Even when she escaped, he wouldn't answer my calls."

"Why the hell not?" Colin came to his feet, the protector vibe set on high.

His immediate, shielding response put a crack in the wall she kept around her heart. "Because she still can't come home."

"Did your parents always play favorites?" He cocked his head. "I have a sister too, older than me. Our parents were pretty even with us, but I know favoritism happens. Human nature to connect with some people and not others."

She knew he was right. It just hurt like hell when that connection was lacking within family. Stress and guilt and blame had snapped those last fragile ties with her father. Although she hoped and wished, she was well aware that the odds were slim to none that she and her father could find a healthy relationship again. "Autumn was barely an adult when she was taken," Summer explained. "I'm six years older and according to my father I should've known better."

"Better than what?" Now Colin stood up and paced. She counted his footfalls, adding them to the tallies running in her head. "I've read the police report, read through the case. Your sister was jumped outside the school where you taught."

"Yes." She closed her eyes, sagging against the back of the couch as the memories flooded over her. "Autumn hit the panic button on her key fob as she tried to fight back. I stepped to the window of my classroom and before I knew it, she'd been stuffed into the back of a pickup truck. One with those lock-down flat-bed covers."

Colin's eyes narrowed and his face flushed with anger.

"Our school officer tried to intervene," she continued. "But he wasn't quick enough."

"Tribal police were first on the scene, right?"

He stopped in front of her and his hand slid over hers. The warmth of his touch stole her voice. She nodded.

"The file says they gave chase," he continued. "Law enforcement across the state was on the lookout for your sister and the truck they were driving." His thumb stroked across her wrist. "If trained police in multiple agencies couldn't find her why would your father think you could?"

"Well, we are the descendants of a famous Crow tracker." One more area where Autumn excelled and she'd disappointed. She swallowed the familiar surge of inadequacy. "He was more furious that I didn't prevent the incident. Schools are suppose to be safe."

Colin snorted. "Lots of places in this world have lost their 'safe' status."

His understanding was a balm to her raw nerves. "Grief is ugly and my dad has lost more than his share through the years. He's stuck, mired in a place I couldn't reach even before we lost Autumn."

"Well, there's sure no chance of a relationship if he won't let you in."

She slipped away from his touch because she wanted to curl into him, breathe in his scent and forget about everything beyond this hotel suite. That was more burden than any bodyguard should bear. "Family dynamics are rarely logical."

"True." He went back to the kitchenette. "Want some tea? I ordered some green tea for you. And honey."

That file on her must be ridiculously detailed. How else would he know her preferences and cater to them? It was more than strange to have someone demonstrating that kind of interest in her, especially over the little things.

Oh, she hadn't been neglected as a child, it had just been ages since anyone outside of Autumn and her students treated her as if she mattered. She hadn't realized how lonely she'd been, even before the kidnapping.

"Summer? Do you want tea?"

"Yes, please." Her cheeks warmed with embarrassment. It wasn't like her to be so distracted. Then again, she'd never been in a situation like this one. "You didn't have to go to all this trouble."

"Don't overthink it. I'm sure it feels weird, but it's standard procedure to keep the client content when a case is in a holding pattern." The coffeemaker filled a mug with hot water and he added the tea bag.

He also ordered room service for breakfast and they talked about mundane topics like pancakes versus waffles until it arrived.

"There's no way we can go *out* looking for Autumn," he said when they finished the spread of eggs, toast, and bacon. "It's probably safe enough to do some independent research. Anything you can tell us about your sister and her habits and preferences, Tyler can put into the system to help the bodyguard assigned to find her."

Hope flooded her system. She was determined to be useful from this point onward, regardless of whether or not her father ever forgave her.

Sipping a second cup of tea, she lost track of time, delighted to share stories about Autumn's dreams and goals. It was heartbreaking to think college and career and a normal life had been stolen from her sister before her life had really begun.

"She was so vibrant," Summer said. "So unstoppable. I can't imagine that changing. She wanted to run triathlons, learn to fly a plane, go sailing."

Colin looked up from the notes he'd been taking. "Sounds like an adventurous girl."

"Absolutely," she agreed. "She loves to learn and experience new things. Somehow our dad doesn't resent her for it. Autumn always had a way of sharing her personal dreams without minimizing what he provided for us."

"Tyler told me there's been no sign of her near your family farm."

"I would've expected her to go there," Summer admitted. "Our family farm is so removed from everything. There aren't any cameras nearby to track her movements. She'd be completely safe out there. Dad doesn't even have a smart phone. There's no internet connection."

Colin's eyebrows rose at that as he added to the notes for his assistant. "Anything else? This is more than we had when Hamilton said her location had been exposed."

Summer shook her head. "If I think of something more, I'll tell you." She tapped the rim of her tea cup. "What if…" She had to steel herself before she could voice the question that had been on her mind since she'd learned that Autumn escaped. "What if being a captive has changed her?"

Colin closed his laptop and set it aside. "I guarantee you, the experience changed her."

"You know what happened? I could guess, though I tried not to. More than once I researched survivor stories, but I just couldn't handle it." Her stomach cramped with the shame that she wasn't strong enough to read about what her sister must have gone through. "Hamilton wouldn't give me full details about Autumn's account of her time."

"It couldn't have been a picnic," Colin said, a frown shading his eyes. He drummed his fingertips on the arm of the chair. "I don't have the facts about what Autumn dealt with or even what she reported. I only know what happened to me."

Shock prickled along her skin. "You were kidnapped?" Was that when he'd been scarred?

"Basically. During my last overseas mission, things went sideways and I was a prisoner of war for a few weeks in Afghanistan."

His tone was too smooth, too calm. She believed the words, but not that he was completely unfazed by talking about it. The polite thing would be to change the subject and let him off the hook. Instead, her curiosity about him trumped manners. "You were in the military?"

"The Army, yes," he answered. "My unit gathered intelligence and promoted a more favorable agenda in local communities."

That was an odd turn of phrase to her ears. It made the work sound a little twisted, though she couldn't pinpoint why. "That type of work left you vulnerable?"

"Not exactly. We worked in small teams, taking the right precautions. All of us were thoroughly trained for our mission." The lines around his mouth deepened, his gaze turned cool and distant. "We knew how to handle ourselves in both clear and questionable circumstances."

She suddenly felt cruel for making him talk about it. "I don't mean to pry."

He held up his hands, a study in carelessness that wasn't any more convincing than his smooth and easy tone. "What else is there to do?"

That was a loaded question and a naughty corner of her mind supplied plenty of other options to pass the time. "Do you think, based on your experience, that Autumn will recover from being held against her will?"

"That's a question only your sister and her shrink can answer." He leaned forward, elbows braced on his knees, his gaze on the glass coffee table between them. "The incident cost me my military career."

She reached out laying her hand on his forearm, cataloging the muscle and sinew, the dusting of hair and the warmth of his skin. "I'm sorry." Such inadequate words to offer a man she was sure had been a hero.

"The Army didn't trust me to do my job after that." His voice was rusty with emotions she couldn't fathom. "That blow was almost worse than being held by the enemy."

She might teach math and stats but she knew her history and kept up on current events. The Taliban wasn't known to abide by the Geneva Convention. American military personnel were used as examples for their cause. Her skin smarted from just the memory of the healed wounds she'd seen earlier. Summer couldn't help wondering what Colin had been like before being a prisoner. More charm or less? Had the man always had an abundance of confidence or did he hide behind it now?

"All I can tell you is that when you see Autumn again, expect the unexpected," he said. "I tried to be tough, to pretend it didn't matter. One more mission off the rails."

"It mattered," she said softly.

His gaze drifted toward some point in his past, a place no one else could reach. He blinked rapidly. "What I'm trying to say is that the details of what happened aren't relevant. Not beyond any specific medical concerns. She survived. I was only a prisoner for a few weeks and the experience altered me. Permanently if you ask the Army or my parents."

"I'll expect the unexpected," she promised. With her hand on his arm, she shifted closer still and pressed her lips to his cheek. "Thank you, Colin."

His gaze turned wary as she sat back again. "For what?"

"For hope." She might find a way to thank him for keeping her alive, but she'd always be in his debt for this very personal insight. "You've given me a boost of faith that I will see my sister again. That we can have a relationship, even if it's a hard path to get there."

CHAPTER 5

DAMN IT. Colin hadn't meant to overshare. He never volunteered information about that last mission. Sure, she'd seen a few of his scars because he'd been careless, but he didn't need to compound matters by explaining his past.

She got up and retreated to her bedroom, leaving him wondering if he was cursed to always watch this woman walk away from him. The view was fabulous, but enough was enough. Desire sizzled under his skin, racing through his system from the places where her hand and lips had touched him to every nerve ending that wanted more of her touches and attention.

How would her mouth fit to his? How would she move under his hands? A rush of similar questions jumbled his thoughts. Not the least bit appropriate and impossible to deny. Apparently his body didn't care about professional boundaries and his brain was quickly running out of excuses to hold the line.

It wasn't enough that she was a client and he was a professional. Up until a few minutes ago, he'd been reminding himself he was too broken, too damaged for a sweet and gentle woman like Summer. Now? Now she'd credited him with giving her hope. That wasn't remotely within his skillset. Since escaping that god-forsaken prison, he'd pursued more destructive behaviors, serving as judge and jury on people doing bad things.

Gamble and Swann had drawn him into the Guardian Agency and saved him from himself. He could admit that now, though he'd resisted for a long time.

Then Summer had come along and singlehand-edly cracked the cinder block wall he hid behind as if it had been nothing more than flimsy veneer. She hadn't flinched at the scars she'd seen. No, she'd had the courage to touch his arm and kiss his cheek. Maybe she wouldn't mind the rest of his wrecked body. The more important parts were still in working order. If she agreed, he had no doubt it would be the best way to while away the hours until Tyler said it was safe to leave.

He gathered up their empty mugs and took them to the kitchenette, considering his approach. Her mug held the trace aroma of her green tea and he smiled. He'd enjoyed spoiling her a bit, arranging for the deliveries overnight so she could have some comfort today. Whatever Hamilton balked at on the expense sheet, Colin could cover. Summer hadn't grown up with much and Colin had grown up with too much.

That's why he'd chosen the Army, to find a level playing field. Though his parents fumed over his decision, it had been the right call for him. Taking this bodyguard job had been the next right move. And that gave him pause as he washed their mugs. This role gave him purpose and just enough structure to keep himself from taking down troublemakers on his own. If anyone at the agency discovered he'd seduced a client under his protection, he'd be fired, no questions asked or third chances given.

Who would tell? asked the devil on his shoulder.

He'd know. A fling with an enticing woman was never really a bad idea. They had the time and the chemistry. At least he was pretty sure about the chemistry. A smart man would find out, test the waters, and have an *adult conversation*, before he made a move that would destroy her trust. Her hope. He was just going to man-up and ask. His days of playing mind games were over.

The door to her bedroom was open. "Summer," he began, crossing the suite. Something outside caught his eye. Not a bird, but a drone, flying straight for the window in her bedroom. "Summer, get down!"

He raced for her room, hurdling the furniture in

his desperation to get her out of sight before the drone spotted her. Only an idiot or someone well-compensated would dare operate a drone this close to the airport. Not a big believer in coincidence, Colin was sure this fly-by was tied to the attempt to derail the case against the Native Mob.

He grabbed her and twisted as he took her to the floor, using his body to cushion hers. "You okay?"

"Yes, but—"

He tucked her right up against the wall between the bed and the chair he'd spent plenty of time in. "Don't move," he whispered. "Think small." He pressed a finger to her lips. "And don't talk."

People were tweaking drones, adding new capabilities all the time and he wasn't taking chances. Better to assume this drone could hear through walls. For that matter, he had to assume the camera was good enough to have caught him leaping through the suite.

He wanted to pull the curtains, but if he did that, it would signal the person operating the drone that this room might be a promising location. Reaching for his cell phone to contact Tyler, he discovered he'd left the device out on the table.

Crap.

He could hear the thing whirring, hovering at the window. The pervy operator had probably peeked into countless windows while searching for Summer.

She curled up tighter and he moved with her, her silky dark hair tickling his cheek.

"Crawl to the bathroom," he whispered. "Close the door if all hell breaks loose."

Her eyebrows lifted toward her hairline, then pinched into a scowl. "I'm not helpless," she said, her voice barely audible.

"Bathroom." He gripped her hands. "Hide now, fight later."

If this was a genuine threat and not some idiot with a peeping-tom complex, they would be hard pressed to make a clean escape if the mob had bribed anyone on the hotel staff. He had to assume the worst to protect Summer effectively. They'd been found by a drone, nothing was outside the realm of possibility.

While she crawled to the bathroom, he stood up, boldly striding closer to the window. The drone wasn't in his direct line of sight, but his suspicions about the pilot's motives were confirmed when the thing turned back.

He walked out of her room, more than a little relieved to reach his phone without incident. He sent a brief text to Tyler with the status and his professional assessment of the situation. Tucking the device into his pocket, he ignored the thing hovering at the window while he packed up his laptop and tucked his revolver into the holster at the back of his belt.

They had to get out of here, but they couldn't

leave anything behind that could be used to track them down or flush them out of hiding.

Everyone working to save the witnesses on this case were convinced the Native Mob had turned someone inside the prosecutor's office. Hell, that's why Hank Patterson had given him his orders in person rather than risk a call or an email. Colin was sure now that extending their stay had been Tyler's attempt to expose the traitor.

Give the kid a bonus. He slung his computer bag over his shoulder and, ignoring the drone, moved toward the bedroom on the opposite side of the suite. Tempting as it had been to settle in and unpack, he'd been diligent about keeping everything in his bag.

Packed in an instant and ready to leave, he hesitated near the couch to see what the drone would do.

His phone rang and Tyler's voice was audible when he accepted the call. "Get out of there!" he shouted repeatedly.

Tyler never panicked. He might get frustrated from time to time, but he kept his cool. Colin dropped his suitcase and hit the deck as something shattered the window behind him. He added sniper to the situation. The small, basic drone hovering outside wasn't packing that kind of firepower.

He shouted for Summer as he ran back toward her room, half-expecting the drone to fly in and follow him through the suite like something out of an action flick. She was crouched in the corner behind the bathroom door, her hands over her ears and the trim rolling suitcase he'd bought for her parked in front of her like a stylish shield.

"This won't be much fun," he said. He picked up her suitcase and held out his free hand to her. "Trust me?"

Her face was pale, but her chin jerked once in the affirmative. "I'm ready."

He doubted either of them were ready for the trek to his car. The parking lot on the other side of the hotel might as well be on the other side of the Rockies right now. "Trust *me*," he repeated. "No one else."

Putting his body between her and the windows, the shuffled her quickly out of the bedroom toward the door of the suite. He grabbed his suitcase on the way, not the least bit surprised when the central window dissolved in a rain of splintering glass.

The odds of surviving this were low unless a gust of wind worked in their favor. In the hallway, he didn't waste time congratulating himself on escaping the room. He pulled the fire alarm and ushered Summer toward the nearest stairwell.

Colin had been watching their six when she screamed. The man from the pawn shop blocked their exit and this time he aimed a gun at her midsection.

"Hand her over and I'll forget you were here," the man said.

The voice was pure Jersey Shore. He was taller and thicker than Colin, with dark hair slicked back from his forehead. He looked as if he'd be fit right in with one of the Italian gangs from the 1930s rather than the mob he was working for today.

"Same goes, Tony." Colin had no idea if that was his name, but Tony fit. Slowly, he reached back for the small revolver.

"No sudden moves." Tony smiled, a creepy expression that showed a gap between his front teeth. "You should just hand over that gun."

Whoever they were, they had excellent communication, Colin thought darkly. "Not gonna happen."

"You sure?" Tony advanced, his weapon digging into Summer's shirt, too close to where he'd cut her yesterday.

"Don't worry," Colin said to Summer. "He wants you alive." He glared at the bastard who kept hurting her. "Isn't that right, Tony? She's got market value and you can use her to draw out her sister."

His wild claims distracted Tony just enough that Summer could twist away, much as she'd done in the pawn shop to avoid the worst of the knife.

Reacting, Tony fired at them. The bullet ricocheted off the block wall of the stairwell and the gunshot echoed in Colin's ears. He tugged Summer aside and kicked out, catching Tony in the groin. The man tumbled backward down the stairs, sliding to an awkward, crunching stop on the first landing.

"Up," Colin ordered and Summer raced with him up to the next floor.

Guests were milling about, half in and half out of their rooms while the fire alarm continued to wail and an automated voice directed them to the stairwell on the opposite side of the elevators.

"What's going on?" a guest asked as they hurried by.

"Fire," Colin replied. "Two floors down. We had to come up this way to get over to a clear stairwell."

The guest gasped and then sniffed the air. "I smell the smoke now."

"Don't waste any time," Summer added as Colin nudged her ahead into the growing throng of people.

"Be on guard," he said at her ear. "A herd doesn't always guarantee safety."

She shot him a look as they moved along. He slid his arm protectively around her waist, one more barrier between her healing wound and the world. Her fingers covered his as they moved with the flow of those obeying the evacuation instructions.

Relief coursed through him when they made it out of the stairwell and into the fresh Colorado air without another confrontation. He mentally crossed his fingers their luck would hold long enough to reach his car.

"Colin." She squeezed his hand as he maneuvered them toward the edge of the crowd. "Look."

He followed her gaze up to see a drone circling

overhead. Mumbling an oath, he wrangled a hat out of his bag and covered his distinctive hair. What could he do to hide her?

"We could separate," she suggested, as if she'd read his mind.

"No." And not just because that kind of tactic had failed her once already.

"I could go hide with the maids or something."

"No," he repeated. He wasn't about to let her out of his sight. "Tony is the only person we know about."

"There's a pilot behind the drone, obviously, and a sniper shooting out windows. Not to mention the person giving the orders," she said.

He stared down at her. "When did you learn my job?"

"Call of Duty," she said, her mouth kicking up at one corner.

A woman who could smile through a potentially deadly situation was a rare gem.

"The kids talk about it all the time," she continued. "I was getting aggravated, not surprised, just aggravated, that they kept choosing the game over homework. So I started playing too."

He was speechless as he processed that information. "We need to get to my car." And hope it hadn't been compromised. The Guardian Agency was big on anonymity, but he hadn't bothered with a fake plate when he'd checked in. Now that the bad guys had connected them, it might be a problem.

Moving along with several others, he kept her as sheltered as possible, his focus cycling between the unseen threat from above and potential threats within the crowd of confused people on the verge of a mass panic.

The cooperative, multi-pronged attack had been more than enough of a surprise for one day. Whoever was bankrolling the effort to wreck the court case had money to burn. He breathed a sigh of relief when they made it to his car without incident and he did a quick sweep of the vehicle to make sure there was neither an obvious threat nor a GPS tag.

"This is your car?" she asked.

The disapproval came through loud and clear. "Got a problem with sports cars?"

"No." She frowned, her arms crossed under her breasts.

He really shouldn't be noticing her breasts right about now. "Good." He stowed their bags and came around to open her door. "Since it's currently your best possible escape route."

"I'll try to enjoy it," she said now, as she had in the suite upstairs. "Thanks."

He wasn't even close to convinced. Closing her door, he hustled around to the driver's side and slipped into the supple leather of the driver's seat.

She was buckled in and posed stiffly, her hands pressed between her knees.

"Problem?" he asked as he started the car.

"No." She sounded prim. "It's a beautiful car."

"Just wait until she gets going." This silver Audi coupe was his passion, his reward, and a pocket of peace whenever things got too crowded in his head. He didn't think sharing any of that would help her relax, so he kept it to himself.

He let the car idle, waiting for another vehicle to leave the lot. Not much cover the way his car stood out from most, but better than nothing. The first responders were closing in and if he didn't move now, they would likely be stuck when the scene was locked down for investigation.

He put the car in Drive and slowly inched along the aisle, mindful of the overwhelmed and displaced people.

Being a prisoner had taught him a new level of patience, and further honed his innate ability to think several steps ahead. He'd had to learn how to read his captors and anticipate what they wanted so he could stay alive while denying them. Those harrowing weeks had also been a crash course in finding egress routes.

He used the same principles now, weaving his way into the flow of traffic headed to the airport. If he was being followed by the drone, it would throw off the pursuit and give them some breathing space.

He wound his way into the short-term parking garage and backed into a space.

"What are you doing?" she asked, still rigid in the seat.

"Waiting to see if we were followed." He didn't mention that he needed a minute to be thankful the car hadn't been disabled or otherwise tampered with. "Do you want to talk about it?"

"Talk about what?" she countered, her gaze on the rows of parked cars.

"Why you hate my car. I daresay it upsets you more than the hotel suite."

"I don't hate your car," she said. "It's very nice."

He was surprised three short words could hold so much judgment. Just when he thought he had a handle on her hang-ups about money and being indebted to others, she threw him another curve ball. He couldn't wait to hear why she disapproved so strongly of the sweet Audi. "You might as well go on and vent it out. We're going to be here a while."

She refused to look at him, her hands gripping the strap of her seatbelt. "We should talk about what happened at the hotel."

That was easy enough. "We were betrayed and attacked. Tyler and others will try to find the compromised link in the chain. End of topic. Now, why do you hate my car?"

"Stop saying that," she complained.

"Then start answering me." Considering what they'd dealt with in their short acquaintance, she should've noticed he could be annoyingly persistent.

She shifted, pinning him with that bold, dark stare. If he'd been a student, he would've caved to whatever she demanded.

"My feelings about your choices have nothing to do with this situation," she said. "You're keeping me safe. I'm grateful."

"My choices?" He nearly laughed in her face. Grateful wasn't what he was after at the moment. "Go on," he prompted.

Her lips pressed tight, then she took a breath. "I'm sure after… after your experiences, you felt it necessary to do something nice for yourself."

"Sweetheart, this perfection of engineering is more than nice."

"I'm not in any position to judge how you spend your money."

"But that's what you're doing. You can't even hide it."

"What do you care about my opinion anyway?"

He shrugged, disguising discomfort with nonchalance. But he'd rather not drift down that path, into his own feelings and issues. Better to keep this chat focused on her problems. "What else is there to do but talk? You're troubled. I've been assigned to alleviate your trouble. Humor me."

She rolled her eyes. "I told you luxury rattles me," she said. "We grew up in a constant state of little to nothing. I didn't know what we were missing, so it wasn't a big deal. I was in college, practically an adult when I learned things this 'nice,'" she used air quotes, "existed. There, are you happy?"

Not at all. "How did you get through college on little to nothing?"

"Scholarships, work study, and debt forgiveness by working off my loans in rural schools."

"Schools on the reservations?" He wanted to understand.

"Yes."

"But your kids have game systems?"

"A few do," she replied. "The rest gravitate to them."

"So is it jealousy or does my obnoxiously expensive investment in this car offend your practical nature?"

Her nose wrinkled and she swore at him. At least he assumed it was swearing, since the words were foreign to his ears.

"I'm not jealous. At the moment, *you* are far more obnoxious than the car."

He laughed, enjoying getting under her skin just enough to open her up so he could understand her better.

She flicked a hand at his laughter as if that was the perfect evidence of his obnoxious nature.

"The car was a splurge," he admitted as his laugher faded. "It's also a glorious reminder that I can go wherever I like whenever I like." He'd needed that more than the mandatory weekly meetings with Army and private sector psychiatrists.

"Any decent car could do that. You came from money."

It sounded like an accusation. "Yes. And I joined the Army to find a place for myself, an identity beyond my father's success. I didn't want to walk in the long shadow of his legacy. It's not that different from you becoming a teacher."

"I teach in order to help," she murmured.

"Exactly."

"What does your father do?"

"He owns hotels. Including the one we just escaped."

"Of course he does." Her laughter started low and gained steam. "That explains a lot."

The merry sound filled the small space and heated his blood. *Down boy.* "To be fair he's an excellent leader and the corporation does give back a hefty percentage to the communities and worthy causes. But I wanted something more basic. A foundation of my own."

She eyed him, one dark eyebrow lifting. "Sure." She circled her finger to indicate the space. "This is all kinds of basic."

He laughed again, enjoying her snarky tone. "Freedom is basic, or should be." That's what the car meant to him. In his opinion, it didn't get more basic than what he'd done with the Army, working up front and behind the scenes in remote areas to help people build secure and better lives. Even now, as a bodyguard assigned to protect strangers, he was on that same general mission.

She nipped her lower lip between her teeth and he could tell her thoughts were on her sister. On how her sister would react and reclaim her life after being under the Native Mob's control and doing who-knew-what for nearly two years. Autumn might not splurge on a high-end car, but Colin would bet his life savings she would act out. It would be an issue for Summer and her father to deal with as a family. It wasn't his place to add to her worries.

He checked the time and figured they were safe, but he decided to call Tyler first.

"About time." The younger man's voice filled the car. "Where are you? I've been juggling a slew of calls from Hamilton and I have Hank Patterson on standby."

"You don't know what happened?" Colin shared a look with Summer.

"I lost you at the airport," Tyler admitted.

That was a surprise. Usually nothing fooled Tyler. "We're in a parking garage," Colin said. "So far no sign that we were followed. What do you know about Tony?"

A brief silence filled the car, then the soft rattle of Tyler's fingers on his keyboard. "Who the hell is Tony?"

"Sorry," Colin said. "He's the guy from the pawn shop. We bumped into him in the hotel stairwell while escaping the drone," Colin explained. "He looked like a Tony to me."

"Got it. I'm pulling up that camera feed again." Tyler was quiet for a moment. "Ouch. You laid a good one on him." Another minute passed as Tyler worked through the man's trail. "He was in the evacuating crowd. I lose him between the lobby and the cameras on the portico. If the police caught him, they're keeping it quiet. The emergency channels are searching for the drone operator. Sounds like they're pinning the whole mess on that one drone."

"Only if the drone was packing guns and missiles," Summer said.

"P-pardon me?" Tyler stuttered.

"She's a gamer," Colin explained. "Call of Duty."

"Nice. Wait a sec. How come I didn't know that?" Tyler wondered aloud.

"You're always telling me everyone has a secret." Colin smothered a laugh. "Are we clear to move out of here yet?"

"You are. You're sure Tony is the same man from the pawn shop?"

"Yes," Colin and Summer confirmed in unison.

Tyler swore softly. "I thought he was working that situation alone."

"I guess they're not taking chances after losing the battle for the first witness," Colin said. When

Summer flinched, he wished he could retract the words. One of the skills he shouldn't have let slide was assessing the impact of every word before he spoke. "Hamilton may have to run this case on remote testimony or the original depositions."

"Based on my crash course in the judicial system, it won't be as strong a case if she does that," Tyler said. "To get the maximum penalties for the two men on trial, they need the witnesses to speak in person in front of the defendants and the jury."

Summer cringed, clearly not eager for that day, despite believing in the necessity of it. He reached over and covered her clasped hands, inordinately pleased when she didn't pull away. If he could spare her the ordeal of walking into that courtroom, he would. He had a feeling she relived that day all the time, with no hope of the recollection making a difference. Testifying could reframe and reset that for her.

"Have you heard anything about my sister?" she asked.

"Not so far. I'm sorry," Tyler replied. "We have our best people looking for her."

Colin gave her trembling hands a squeeze. "Do you think the kidnappers will walk if she isn't in court?" He asked the question so Summer wouldn't have to.

"Crash course, remember. I'm no law expert, but Hamilton seems confident she'll get a conviction, even if she can only submit the video of Autumn's initial interviews and deposition."

"All right," Colin said, eager to get moving again. "We'll find a new hiding place and be in touch."

"Do me a favor and hide as close to Eagle Rock as you can," Tyler said. "Send all further updates through Patterson, in person if possible."

Colin stared at the display that showed Tyler's phone number. "Seriously?"

"Seriously. When I'm confident about the communication again, you'll be the first to know."

The call ended and Colin and Summer were left staring at each other, hands still joined. There were tears swimming in her dark eyes. She blinked several times before they could spill over. Her strength of will impressed him.

He reached up and slid his fingers through the heavy silk of her black hair, then grazed the shell of her ear, the line of her jaw to her chin. *Can I kiss you?* He wasn't sure if he'd said the words aloud or if the question merely rattled around his head. Either way, she came to him, her hands cupping his face as she pressed her lips to his.

The contact zipped through his bloodstream, lighting up every nerve. Even the places he'd thought were burned out. Fireworks exploded behind his closed eyes when her lips parted and her tongue stroked over his. The taste of her roused a deep hunger that couldn't be fully satisfied here in his car.

For the first time in his life, he wished he drove a van.

He let her go when she eased back into her seat, her fingertips dragging across the whiskers he hadn't had time to scrape away before the drone attack. He should say something. Beg for more. Explain that he didn't do things like this with clients.

"I, um…" Great. One kiss had rendered him incoherent. True, the kiss had been that good. Still.

"Thank you, Colin. For protecting me."

"That isn't how any of my other clients react."

One eyebrow arched and her mouth curved into a shrewd smile that could only be described as possessive. "Good."

Something had changed. In her head or his. Maybe it was surviving. Life threatening experiences often gave people a new outlook. He wasn't sure about what it meant to Summer, but his body wanted his brain to analyze something different. Not her, not what he hoped would be their first kiss rather than their only kiss.

"How far is it to Eagle Rock?" she asked. "At the speed limit."

The question reset his priorities and the clarification made him smile. "Ten to twelve hours, based on stops and traffic."

"I guess we'd better get moving," she suggested.

He was reconsidering the 'sweet' label he'd

applied to her. The woman had a sassy edge he could get used to. "Right."

He started the engine and put the car in gear, moving cautiously on his way out of the parking garage. Tyler's extreme precautions were unexpected and he was struggling to put everything into the right context while his body hummed with the after effect of that kiss.

She twisted in her seat, checking behind them, and then the mirrors as well.

"No one is on us yet," he said as he paid the fee.

"But you expect it."

"I'd be a lousy protector if I didn't," he pointed out. "Relax, Summer. I've got this." He made an exaggerated effort to check each of his mirrors as they drove away from the airport.

She stopped fidgeting. "It's either in the blood or the upbringing, but I have a *need* to be helpful and useful."

Her shy admission went straight through him. "All right. Be helpful and fill me in," he said. "You were raised on the reservations and you teach in the school system now. What have you heard about the Native Mob, trafficking, or other organized crime?"

"Not enough before Autumn was taken," she said. "I mean, I've known for years that women have been disappearing from the reservations. Too often the disappearances aren't even reported and when they are, real investigations are rare. Most of the missing women never come home." She rubbed her arms as if she felt a chill. "Some cases get closed when hunters find remains."

Until this case, he'd had no idea what the tribal communities were dealing with. "And after the kidnapping?" he asked.

"I did more research," she admitted.

"Lay it on me," he urged. "We have a long drive ahead of us."

Aiming for Eagle Rock felt a little like driving into the danger zone, but if that's what Tyler recommended, so be it. Colin wouldn't mind having Hank Patterson and his crew at his back when Tony and his associates caught up with them again.

Since leaving the Army, Colin usually preferred to handle things on his own, fewer people to worry about getting caught in the crossfire. But after the drone encounter, a little support sounded like a great idea.

He glanced over to see Summer plucking at her seatbelt, though she had yet to say a word. "Was the research too boring or too vague?" he prompted.

"Turned out to be too dangerous," she replied.

Her voice had faded to a rasp and when he spared her another glance, he caught her wiping away a tear. It wasn't ideal to handle an emotional meltdown while keeping an eye out for danger on the road, but no case ever followed a perfect script.

"I'm listening," he said. "Talk to me."

CHAPTER 6

SUMMER DID *NOT* WANT to have this conversation. Bad enough her father dumped all of the blame about Autumn on her shoulders and was bent on hating her and punishing her forever for wrecking the fragile family they'd been.

Now Colin would see the real her. Once he learned her part in all of this, he'd hate her too. That fabulous kiss—the best of her life—would become a bittersweet memory. Or just bitter.

She'd been all judgmental about the over-the-top suite and his impossible car, all because she didn't deserve to enjoy nice things. Not after the massive mistakes she'd made. Mistakes that took an unspeakable and violent toll on her sister.

When Autumn had escaped her captors in Eagle Rock, Summer had been desperate to see her again, to apologize, to do anything possible to make up for the horrors her sister had suffered. Dread had paced that desperation stride for stride. She'd wanted to explain everything, but both the prosecutor and Autumn had refused a reunion. If—when—Autumn learned why she'd been taken, she'd never give Summer a second chance to be a good sister.

"If you're not ready—"

"No. I'm past ready." Maybe it was better to talk in the car, when his attention was divided and she couldn't try and distract either of them with another kiss. When Colin leveled the full force of those changing hazel eyes on her, she couldn't keep her thoughts lined up in an orderly fashion. He scrambled her senses with a look, or that deep laugh. And when he touched her she wanted to crawl right into his arms and stay there forever.

"There's a reason I'm all weird about money these days. I mean part of it was growing up poor, but there's more."

"Beyond the guilt of enjoying life when you don't know if your sister is able to do the same thing?"

"Do you see right through everyone?" she asked with an embarrassed sigh.

"Most of the time," he admitted.

"Great." She watched the scenery for a minute, doing simple equations about miles traveled and miles to go as she gathered her courage. "Recently, I've learned not to trust people with money. On the reservation, blatant wealth is rarely displayed."

"You're saying people don't vacation in high-end hotels or drive sexy sports cars?"

Sexy? Yes, that fit him to a tee. How did manage to he make her want to laugh at a moment like this? "Not often. The past few years I've watched people who came into money use it to manipulate the system and influence my students."

"You mean the gangs were recruiting."

"Yes. Game systems for select people, laptops for others, it goes on and on."

"Bribes that drew in fresh blood."

"Exactly." She pushed her hair back from her face. "There's a low level of gang action and corruption all the time. Everywhere. It was that way when I was in school. The gangs on the reservations have changed, becoming more dangerous than ever, even amid the small, local crews. A few years back, one of my students was getting caught up and dragged in. I tried to head it off, getting more involved with her and doing deep research on the kids harassing her. The whole thing blew up in my face. When I took my findings to the principal for help, I was told I was overstepping. I argued, loudly, and he suspended me for a week."

"That sounds pretty corrupt," he said.

"I agree. It was bad news for my students too," she grumbled. "Especially the one at risk. Without me around, my student was bullied and jumped after class. She wound up in the hospital. I convinced her to press charges and then my classroom was vandalized. There were death threats in my mailbox and on my phone. I refused to back down and they took Autumn."

"You believe they took Autumn because you were getting too close to exposing the gang?"

"I do." Misery swamped her, but she wanted him to hear it all. "I think the locals were working for someone higher up the food chain and those men kidnapped my sister as retaliation. I cost them one young woman so they took Autumn in her place. I'm the reason she suffered. She'll never forgive me for that. She shouldn't."

Her hand was suddenly enveloped by his. The gesture surprised her and she laced her fingers though his, greedily taking every comfort he offered.

"None of this is your fault, Summer. Trying to do the right thing backfires sometimes. Life sucks that way. But you did the right thing," he said.

"How can you be so cavalier about my responsibility here?" Her stubborn streak had brought harm to her only sister. "Is backing the client an unwritten rule of the bodyguard code or something?"

"No, backing good people is a smart general rule for life." He checked his mirrors. "I look at you and I see a good person in trouble. I see a good person who's been hurt. Not in the same way as your sister, but hurt takes a toll in any form." He glanced over at her, a ghost of a smile on his lips. "And I see a good person who misses her family."

She appreciated his attempt to encourage her. If only she felt worthy of that kindness and compassion. Not only from him, but from her sister. "You aren't repulsed?"

He gave her hand a gentle squeeze. "That's what you expected? You have been dealing with this by yourself for too long."

Maybe he was unique. Or maybe life had warped her dad's outlook more than she wanted to admit. Either way, she had not expected this gracious acceptance. "You told me to expect the unexpected when I see Autumn again."

"And I meant it. You love her, but she might want to test that, to see if you'll love her after her ordeal."

"Did you do that?"

"Of course," he confessed. "Between the Army shrinks and the family counselor, I was a complete pain in the ass. I pushed everyone away, went off the rails to get some space, but eventually someone talked sense into me."

His candor was refreshing. "Autumn and I used to talk sense into each other." She poked at a ragged cuticle on her thumb nail. "I'm not sure we'll ever find our way back there."

"Give it time," he said with another check of the mirrors.

"What if it's on me? What if I can't look her in the

eye and tell her I'm sorry?" She closed her eyes tight and took a deep breath. "Even if I could go back in time, I wouldn't change my attempt to save that student. I've struggled to reconcile that since the moment I saw them dragging Autumn away." She swiped at another tear that slipped through her control. "It is the worst feeling."

"I'm sure it is," Colin soothed. "You can't change what happened, you can only move forward. I can't imagine how you feel having witnessed that."

"Helpless," she said. "And helpless sucks."

"I'm aware. Being a prisoner in a dirt hole is a pretty helpless feeling," he said. "But it became one of the reasons I'm out here doing what I do now."

"Please tell me another reason." She needed the distraction, needed something to pull her out of this emotional pit.

"Well, at the top of the list, the Army won't take me back. Everyone's afraid I'll snap," he said. "Even the agency. I have to accept that they might not be wrong."

It wasn't all that reassuring, but she couldn't fault his honesty or the self-deprecating way he shared himself so openly with her. "Do you admit that to all your clients?"

His grin was fast and sharp. "Only the ones who kiss me."

"You're incorrigible."

"Now you're getting it." He rolled his shoulders

and settled back into the seat. "So is that your darkest secret? You feel responsible that the gang used your sister as payback rather than come directly at you."

"Yes. Dad might not know the details, but he knows I failed to keep those men off my sister. That's all that matters to him."

"Sounds like your dad has his own issues," Colin observed.

"Everyone is dealing with something," she murmured.

"True," he agreed. "Most of the time that makes me feel better."

He had a point, she thought, shifting her gaze to the rugged scenery surrounding them. Everyone carried around guilt. She supposed it was just a matter of varying degrees and circumstance.

"How are your stitches holding up?" he asked, breaking several minutes of companionable silence.

"I'm feeling good," she said. They drove along, each in their own thoughts for several more miles.

"If you had all the money in the world, what would you do?" he asked.

She didn't take that kind of question lightly. Growing up on a farm that barely made ends meet had stunted the healthy development of big dreams. "I'd still teach," she admitted at last. "I enjoy the process and the kids. Most days," she added. "It would be nice to move Dad to a better farm, although he'd probably hate me for that too. After all of this, I would definitely invest in programs to mitigate crimes against women and empower survivors. I guess to have unlimited resources and still want to do basically the same things sounds small-minded."

"Not at all. You sincerely want to help people," he observed. "That's a good thing."

"It hasn't worked out well for Autumn, but with luck we can turn that around," she said. "Eventually."

She studied his sharp profile, her lips warming at the memory of their kiss. Golden highlights in his hair glinted in the sunlight. Watching him, she could almost see the wheels turning. She'd bet all of that hypothetical windfall that he'd been asking questions to distract her while he worked through some deep thoughts of his own.

Worried they'd been found, she swiveled around. "Did they catch up to us?"

"Take it easy." He smiled, keeping his eyes on the road. "No one's on our tail yet."

"What kind of plan are you brewing up?" she asked. At his quizzical glance, pointed at his face. "You're not the only one who can read people."

"I'm innocent," he joked. "We'll do exactly as Tyler directed, behaving ourselves all the way into Eagle Rock. There, we'll keep a low profile and wait it out until Hamilton needs you in court."

"Before all of this I was nervous. Now I can't wait to testify against those bastards."

"Fierce." He clearly approved. "That bodes well for everyone."

"I don't suppose your family has a hotel near Eagle Rock."

"So you did enjoy yourself after all." His low laughter filled the car.

"That robe was so soft," she gushed.

"I hate to disappoint you, but even if we did have a property in the area, after what just happened, it wouldn't be a good choice."

"You're the expert." She wasn't sure if it was the stress or the sunshine, but she was getting sleepy. She let her head fall back against the seat.

He reached over and slipped his hand into hers again. "It would only take a phone call to hook you up with one of the robes," he said.

She gazed at him, more than a little surprised by the offer. "You'd do that?"

"For you? In a heartbeat."

His immediate and intense response surprised her. Then again, he was a man of decisive action. A trait that had saved her a few times already.

"Do you know anything about Eagle Rock?" she asked.

"Never seen more than the airfield. The aerial view was pretty," he told her. "Why?"

"I've always wondered why Autumn made her escape there."

"She probably picked up on the vibe that someone

would be willing to help," he said. "Just like you wanted to help your student, Marnie, the cafe owner, was willing to help your sister."

"Do you think we can meet Marnie?"

"I can see about working that out with her bodyguard. Don't count on it right away. I'll need to get a feel of the area first and no one wants the top witnesses exposed to more danger. We have no idea how long the mob will wait before coming at you again."

"Tyler said Marnie was safe now."

"That may only be due to where she is and the number of eyes on her between my agency and Patterson's crew. How do you feel about camping?" he asked.

It took her a second to shift gears along with the change of subject. "I've done plenty of it though I'm not a huge fan," she admitted.

He aimed another sideways glance her way. "So you don't like roughing it but you don't like being spoiled rotten in a hotel suite. Middle of the road it is," he teased.

She laughed at herself. "That's me, Average Jane."

"Hardly."

Her heart fluttered at what probably wasn't a compliment. She really needed a nap to regain her perspective. It was as though she'd kissed him and now a part of her—the part that didn't want to think about more serious issues—wanted to craft romantic fantasies complete with roses and sappy lyrics.

"Use my phone," he suggested. "Check out the motel options in Eagle Rock and bookmark a couple that appeal to you."

She did as he asked, all the while fighting the awareness that what she found most appealing was being with him. His voice, his outlook, all of it held enormous appeal. It was absurd to be this enamored with a man she barely knew, but something about him resonated within her.

Some deep facet of herself recognized its match in Colin and she already worried that new part of her would be crushed when their time together was done.

CHAPTER 7

TWILIGHT WAS GIVING way to full dark when Colin's instincts prickled to life. Traffic had been less and less frequent for hours, yet there was a set of head-lights in his rear view that crept close and fell back, never moving to pass.

"Here we go," he murmured. Summer was dozing in the passenger seat and he hated to wake her. Using the hands-free option and voice commands, he called Patterson.

The former SEAL picked up on the second ring. "You made good time," Hank said. "I'll send Bear over—"

Colin interrupted him. "We won't be there tonight. I've got a tail." He gave Hank his position on the highway.

"You're only a few hours out."

"If I stay this course," Colin said. "I need to know

where we can lay low once I lose this guy." He'd changed license plates the first time they'd stopped for gas, knowing it wasn't likely to hamper the team hunting Summer for long.

"I'll get you the information. And I'm sending out a few men." Hank rattled off three different state roads. "Got that?" he asked.

"Yes," Summer replied. "I know those routes."

"Good. Stick with them. It gives you options and makes finding you easier if you can't make contact. I'll keep your assistant up to date."

"Thanks," Colin said as the headlights surged up closer to his bumper and fell back again. "Quiet time's over."

He ended the call and focused on what he had to do to avoid certain disaster. In the passenger seat, Summer was fully awake, her hands clasped in her lap. "I've got this," he assured her. He accelerated to get some space from the trailing car.

"I know." Her voice was cool, detached. "If I can help, say so."

"Will do."

The car matched his speed, running so close he couldn't see the headlights anymore. The driver eased up and then jerked into the left lane and came up alongside them. The passenger window was down and Colin recognized Tony's face in the dim light behind a menacing gun.

Knowing his car, Colin stomped on the brakes a

split-second before Tony fired. The bullets flew off into the night as Colin pulled in tight behind the killers. They were driving a newer muscle car with what appeared to be a rental car bar code on the rear window. Without significant upgrades Tony's vehicle was no match for his Audi.

Colin swerved back into the other lane before Tony could fire into his windshield. He didn't expect to bring the car through this without a scratch, but he planned to do his best to mitigate any damage.

The driver of the muscle car overcompensated and skidded into the loose gravel at the shoulder. Colin used his advantage and opened up the Audi to fly along the deserted ribbon of highway. Summer's only reaction was to gasp, her knuckles white as the needle on his odometer edged toward one hundred miles per hour. Then over.

The sports car had been engineered for this. Hugging the road, the Audi carved the gentle, uneven curves as efficiently as if they were on a straightaway. The other car was persistent and it required passing up two exits before they had enough space to escape the highway unseen.

"Nicely done," Summer said.

He went warm all over at her praise and the reaction surprised him a little. "Thanks. Did Hank send those suggested places to stay?"

She picked up his phone and checked the alerts.

"He did. If you want, we're close enough that we could stay on Crow land."

Was that a test? "As much as I'd like to see where you grew up, I'd rather know someone we trust has our backs."

"I won't argue with that."

When he glanced her way, she was wearing that feminine smile again, the expression that first appeared after she'd kissed him. It gave him hope that more kisses were on the agenda once they were off the road for the night.

SUMMER GUIDED Colin through the back roads to an aging motel on one of the routes Hank suggested. It was late when they stopped for the night and she was hungry, but not for the sandwiches and colas Colin picked up at the truck stop across the street before they checked in.

She wanted the man.

Maybe it was adrenaline or some new-found appreciation for the temporary nature of life. Her heart still kicked from how expertly he'd overcome the trouble on the road. Watching him handle his car made her want to have those hands on her. That was basic, primal sex appeal and attraction. But the way her lips tingled every time she thought of their kiss this morning, she suspected it was far more serious.

Like a sudden-onset addiction for one particular man with ginger hair and a long, confident stride. She was torn between wanting to talk and wanting to jump him. Surely if she jumped him they could talk later.

They entered their room and she nearly laughed. Nothing like the suite where her day had started, a small, worn nightstand was wedged between two double beds. A table and two chairs were shoved into the corner and the mirror over the sink was chipped at the corners.

"It's clean," she said, walking over to set the food on the table. And they weren't being shot at or under attack. "And it's safe. Thank you, Colin."

He turned from locking the door and arched an eyebrow. "Seriously?" He shook his head at the strange paisley print on the bedspreads. "I'll never figure you out."

"It could do with a fluffy robe, sure, but it beats roughing it."

He laughed as he tucked their bags into the narrow space between the bed and the bathroom wall. "I'd like to get word to Hank. It would save his men some time." He planted his hands on his hips and eyed the phone on the nightstand.

"Think it takes a credit card?" she asked, turning away from the view of his enticing chest. He'd touched her frequently throughout the day in a caring manner, but he hadn't given her any obvious indication that he wanted another kiss. Or any of the crazy things plaguing her thoughts.

"I paid an extra twenty bucks at the desk to cover incidentals," he said. He looked around the modest room. "I don't see anything else here to spend money on. Let's hope the phone falls under that umbrella."

She unpacked the food while he gave Hank the update, but she still wasn't hungry for food when he joined her. He might very well be starving, having done all the hard work to get them this far. Choosing a bottle of water, she opened it and poked at her sandwich.

"Something wrong?" He'd downed half of his meal already and looked ready for more.

"It's fine." She forced herself to take a hearty bite and tried to look happy about it. Tired of wasting time, she shoved out of her chair and pulled the curtains across the window.

"Summer?"

Her eyes on him, she pulled her shirt off over her head and reached for the button of her jeans. She watched as his jaw clenched. "For tonight can we forget we're bodyguard and client?" She flipped the button open and lowered her zipper. "Unless you're not interested."

He was up on his feet, staring at her. "I'm interested. But you need to be sure."

"I'm sure. Come here and find out."

He stepped up and kissed her, his hands in her

hair tilting her face to take the kiss deeper. She reveled in it, eager for more. Lifting the hem of his shirt, he stopped her, his hands hard and unyielding.

"Turn out the light first."

"No."

"It's ugly. My body is a mess."

"I saw your back this morning," she reminded him. "I can handle it."

"Maybe I can't." His hand skated gently up and down her arm. "You're so beautiful and I'm...I'm not."

"Do you want to see all of me?"

"God, yes."

She pushed up on her toes and kissed the strong column of his throat. "Good. Then the lights stay on."

He groaned. "One condition." He cupped her backside in his hands, squeezed. "If it's too much, you'll tell me."

"Deal."

Finally, he was kissing her again, his lips and tongue and teeth priming her for more. She wriggled out of her jeans and though her bra and panties weren't anything fancy, he seemed enthralled.

His shirt came off at last and she wanted to weep over the evidence of what he'd endured in that prison. Instead she gloried in the strength of his muscles under those healed wounds, her hands skimming over his skin, learning what he enjoyed.

He drew her to the bed and traced the edge of her bandage. "You're sure you're fit enough for this?"

"Well, if I pass out or something, I know you can deal with it."

He chuckled, and then there was no more talking, only sighs and gasps and surges of pleasure as they explored each other thoroughly. She kissed each and every mark of his courage and bravery in the worst possible conditions. The man was a hero. He might not believe her words, so she let her body convince him until they were both too sated for anything but sleep.

THE NEXT MORNING Colin stepped out of the room, his arm around Summer's waist. Donning his sunglasses, he noticed a black SUV backed into a space facing their room. A tall, fit man leaned against the driver's door, his eyes shaded by a ball cap. Colin had the feeling every detail was being catalogued, filed away for a future report or reference.

"Hank's man," he murmured to Summer.

"You're sure?"

Anyone else watching them so intently would be shooting by now. Keeping his arm around her, they crossed the aged blacktop parking lot. The man met him halfway and stuck out his hand. "Colin Hazard?" When Colin nodded, he introduced himself. "Axel Svenson. Call me Swede."

The nickname fit the man's fair hair and blue eyes.

"This is Summer Curley," Colin added. "We appreciate the assist," he said. He was not about to apologize for the few hours of indulgence and quality rest he'd enjoyed with Summer overnight. Guilt wasn't anywhere close to the top of the list of feelings coursing through his system this morning. "Can I buy you a coffee before we head out?"

"No thanks," Swede said. A knowing smile lifted the corner of his mouth. "I'm set. You two ready to roll?"

"We are," she answered for them. "Has there been any trouble in Eagle Rock overnight?"

"Not that I've heard, but we're all on high alert. Pretty sure after the situation with Marnie that these guys know where to look for you."

"Got it." With another handshake, he guided Summer back to his car.

Once they were underway, her nerves were too obvious to ignore. "Don't keep it bottled up now," he said. "What's on your mind?"

She fidgeted in her seat. "Tell me why we're going right into a place where they expect us to be?"

"So we can control the situation," he said. "Usually I handle things on my own, just me and the client, with Tyler chiming in when needed. This case has been different from the start. In part because the U.S. Attorney is calling the shots. If my counterpart and the U.S. Attorney are content keeping Marnie in Eagle Rock, it seems smart to follow their example. Patterson has the best men in the business—"

"Second best," she said. "But I might be biased."

He felt his face heating with a mix of pride and embarrassment and she laughed as his ears reddened. He cleared his throat. "My point is Patterson also has enough top people in the area to make sure you and Marnie get to the trial."

She accepted that and the conversation turned back to stories of her childhood in this rugged and beautiful part of the country. Listening to her talk was a treat and he soaked up every insight she gave him along the way.

It was just past noon when they finally rolled into Eagle Rock. Knowing how much it meant to Summer, he drove down Main Street, passing Marnie's cafe. It gave Colin a chance to get a feel for the town layout. They might be on Hank's turf, but protecting her was his job, obviously. Doubly so after last night. Whatever happened after this, a part of him would always be hers.

Swede trailed them for the brief tour of Eagle Rock, parking beside them when they stopped at Ruby's Bed and Breakfast, according to an earlier text message from Hank. Swede rolled down his window and Colin did the same. "Hank has everything set for you here. We'll have people around, close enough if you need a hand."

"Appreciate it," Colin said. Summer added her thanks as well.

Logically, Colin was aware that keeping a client alive would never balance the scales for the people he lost in that ambush in Afghanistan. That was done, a tragedy he'd never be able to change. But he was learning to cope with it. Learning to relish living again. Every good feeling he had was now tied to Summer and her concerted efforts to enjoy the good moments too.

Outmaneuvering and outwitting a few bastards abusing women wouldn't hurt either. *That* would give him a chance let loose with some of this anger that continually plagued him.

"It's a nice town," she said. "Clean and trendy. I didn't expect trendy," she said.

"Has to be with the frequent celebrities that come through," he said. "Is that going to trip you up?"

"No more than anything else," she said with a radiant smile.

That smile threw a soft-blur filter over the rest of the world and at the center of everything was this wonderful woman. "I see why your students like you," he said.

"What do you mean?"

Great. Now he'd spoken without thinking and he had to back it up. "You're different," he began, his thoughts scrambling. "You willingly own your issues. Do you know how rare that is?"

"Typically, self-awareness is part of being a grown up."

He laughed. "Then I have met some very tall children in my life." He looked around, feeling more exposed, inside and out. "Let's get checked in."

"Let's." She took her suitcase, a tempting smile on her lips.

He couldn't wait to taste her again for the pure joy of it. She was all kinds of luxury even if she wasn't entirely comfortable with wealth. His or anyone else's. Once they had their key, they went up to the room and stowed their bags. With the bed and breakfast schedule and a map of the town, they headed back downstairs.

"Why don't we leave the car and walk to the café," he suggested.

She curled her arm around his. "It would be nice to walk a bit."

It was a short walk and he took an immediate liking to Marnie's tidy place. The café fit the vibe of the town perfectly and even in this off time after lunch, locals were lingering over coffee and thick slabs of pie. Colin wondered what on earth would've made the kidnappers stop at this particular establishment.

The little he knew about traffickers didn't fit with this sort of place. Too cozy. Too personal. He'd seen the pictures of the men and they would've stood out like raw beef at a vegan convention. He couldn't turn off the need to puzzle it out. It felt like a critical piece of saving Summer was learning what brought her sister here.

The hostess seated them in a booth near the window and brought over two glasses of water. Summer ordered apple pie and a coffee. Colin chose cherry pie. While they waited, he could practically see Summer thinking the same things he'd been thinking.

"You see it too, don't you?"

She bit her lip. "The men who took Autumn would never fit in here. Not in a hundred years. For that matter, it's hard to see my sister fitting in with this crowd."

"Why not?" He quickly recalled what she'd told him about her sister so far.

"She's always been a little wild. Happier outside than indoors. She'd rather feel the wind in her hair and drink from a creek then sip filtered water from a nice glass."

Colin watched Summer's fingertips trail over her glass and was transported back to last night when those hands had drifted over his skin and scars. He had taken so much abuse in prison and she'd put her gentle touch on every brutal reminder.

"What are you thinking about?" she asked.

"Not safe for work," he quipped. "Or small-town cafés."

She blushed. "You can tell me later."

"In detail." He leaned forward. "Want a preview?" he asked, his voice low. She nodded and leaned close. "I'm thinking how nice it will be to have your hands on me again."

It was harder to see on her golden skin, but the sweetest glow colored her cheeks.

He shifted the topic to reclaim his focus. There was a very important reason to be here. "So if we agree the two criminals would never venture in here, we have to assume your sister manipulated them somehow."

"That's a given," Summer said. "I grew up with her, I know what she can do when she's determined."

He mulled that over. What did it say about a trafficking operation that the captive had exerted such effective control over her handlers? He knew it could be done. Hell, he'd done it himself. In his case, the guards had full authority over everything he did. It was their schedule that dictated his life, his survival.

"I found a measure of control in how much I cooperated," he heard himself say. "And that wasn't one hundred percent of the time. I had to learn how to read my guards. If they'd wanted me dead I wouldn't be here. Trust me, *that* is a sobering awareness when playing a slow burn mind game while you're perpetually exhausted and in pain."

Summer reached across the table and touched his hand, tracing a scar. "I'm glad you made it."

Her patient touch was all it took to draw him

back from those hard memories. The pie and coffee arrived and she released him, he tried not to resent the friendly intrusion.

"I can't figure out why the three of them were even in this town," she said as she placed her napkin in her lap.

"That is the question. If Hamilton has a theory, she hasn't put it in any file Tyler or I have read." He had to give that more thought.

"Do you want to speak with Marnie before we go?" he asked, polishing off his cherry pie.

She hesitated. Looking down at the last bite of crust on her plate, she gave her head the tiniest shake. "I don't. Not today. We'll be here for a few days, right?"

"Looks that way." Possibly up to a week of Summer's sweet and sexy company in a quaint bed and breakfast with a beautiful town to explore while they waited. It would be almost like a vacation. The best of his life if he played his cards right.

Summer's lips pursed. "I'm just not ready to face the person who rescued Autumn when I'm the reason she was taken."

He'd been giving that some thought too. "The gangs moved on your sister awfully quick." That was the impression he got from the report Hank had given him as well as the additional information Summer had shared. It was a brutally efficient strategy to target an innocent loved one instead of launching a direct attack on the person involved.

But Summer hadn't caved to the threats. He wondered if the gang had already been looking at Autumn for reasons Summer didn't know about.

He paid the check and they headed back, taking their time on the way back to Ruby's.

"How long do you think it will be until the trial?" she asked.

"Tyler thinks it will be least another week," he said.

"And you're just going to stick with me until that happens? You could turn me over to Hank's crew."

"Sorry. The job means you're stuck with me," he said. "I care about what happens to you. That's partly the job and partly because I like you."

Colin couldn't recall the last time he'd said that to a woman. He wasn't the sort of person who went around spewing his feelings. Feelings were dangerous territory that consistently tripped him up since his time as a prisoner, but she brought this side of him closer to the surface. She made him feel safe enough to say what was on his mind.

He understood her reservations about seeing her sister. Or speaking to Marnie. He understood that conflict better than most people would. It was more than just guilt, it was knowing your actions had unintended, irreversible consequences.

Summer's head was on a swivel. Passersby might

assume she was charmed by the town but he suspected it had more to do with wondering how her sister navigated the same street.

"What would your sister think of Eagle Rock?" he asked.

Summer bumped her shoulder to his. "You read my mind." She smiled at him. "Autumn would have loved this town. It's unique. There's something to see on every corner, and the people seem friendly."

"Friendly enough to take a chance on escaping?"

"Apparently so," she said.

They were a block away from the bed and breakfast and his mind drifted back to why the kidnappers would risk driving through. There were cowboys and retired military everywhere. He would bet nine out of ten people were carrying weapons or had them within easy reach.

Either Autumn's kidnappers were brash men traveling through with a purpose or they were fools. Colin knew which he would prefer facing. A fool was unpredictable, but a brash man could often be turned on himself and become his own worst enemy.

They started across the street when the storefront window behind him shattered. Reacting automatically, he shoved Summer around the corner and protected her with his body. Another gunshot cracked through the air.

Someone was firing from a rooftop, he decided, based on the sound and angle. The gunfire had drawn plenty of attention and people were shouting and pointing. The safety of others wasn't his concern, only Summer. He pulled his handgun from the holster and slowly peeked around the corner, searching for the shooter.

He took another step and got tagged when the sniper fired again, chipping the brickwork on the building.

"You're bleeding," Summer exclaimed.

"It'll heal." How in the hell was he going to get Summer out of here?

An SUV skidded to a stop, Swede behind the wheel, giving them the escape they needed. He shoved her into the back seat and followed right behind.

Swede took them around to the rear of the bed and breakfast and stopped. "It's clear," he said.

"Thanks." Colin sat up, helped Summer do the same. "Again." He was starting to understand why Tyler wanted them here in Eagle Rock.

"It's what we do. We should have the sniper shortly."

"Great. Keep me posted." He smiled at Summer and found her glaring daggers at him for some reason. "What?"

"You've been shot!"

CHAPTER 8

Swede swiveled around in the driver's seat. "How bad?"

"It's nothing," Colin said. "A graze. We're good."

She nearly punched him when he reached for the door. "He's bleeding through the shirt." But Colin was out of the car and waiting for her.

Up front, Swede chuckled. "Call if it's worse than he thinks."

"Sure." With a thank you, she hopped out of the SUV. "What are you thinking?"

"I have a first aid kit upstairs. I'd rather get a look at it before I panic," he said.

She fumed. The man had been shot while protecting *her*. She was impressed and appalled all at once. "How about you let me look at it," she said when they reached their room.

"Whatever."

"Into the bathroom," she ordered. She stopped to root through his suitcase for the first aid kit.

"You're bossy."

"Yeah, well you're being dumb." With as much care as possible, she stripped away his T-shirt. Even angry and worried, it was impossible to ignore his sculpted chest.

"Tempted?"

"By many things," she replied, coolly. Numerous holes pierced the fabric where the bullet had tracked through, scoring his upper arm. "No salvaging this," she said, tossing it into the trash can under the pedestal sink.

Taking a look at the wound, it wasn't as bad as she'd originally thought. She cleaned away the debris and assessed it again.

"Do you have much experience with this?" he asked.

"Are you kidding? I grew up on the reservation, of course I do."

His grin flashed. "That wild?"

She shook her head. "More like that remote. Most of the time we took care of things on our own." She looked through the kit for antiseptic ointment. "Waiting for a doctor most of the time didn't make sense."

"You're frowning."

"I can't decide if you should have stitches," she said.

"Will you put them in?" he asked, his grin on full display.

"I can," Swede said from the doorway.

Summer spun around. "How'd you get in here?"

"Ruby," the other man replied. "I wanted you to know we caught the shooter. He's in the sheriff's custody. Joe and his dog, Six took him down. He's pretty scared right now. While scared doesn't always equal cooperative it's a good start. After what happened in Denver, we're prepared for anything this side of Armageddon."

"Good," Colin said. "Let me know if he gives you anything to work with."

"You got it." Swede leaned over and checked the wound. "I'd skip the stitches, but that's me."

"I'm sorry to bring such trouble here," she said.

Both men shook their heads at her. "You aren't the problem," Colin assured her.

Swede leaned against the doorway. "Have you spoken to your sister since she escaped at Marnie's?"

"No, I haven't had the opportunity. Why?"

Something unspoken and significant passed between Swede and Colin. She didn't feel judged, but it was unnerving to realize how far out of her element she was. Oh the town might be nice and the company intriguing, but the situation was well beyond her. If she had known anything about investigations or criminal enterprise it was possible her sister would never have been in jeopardy.

"What aren't you telling me?" she demanded.

Colin indicated Swede should start. "Between the Guardian Agency and the Brotherhood Protectors our surveillance and data experts have been doing all we can to sort out why this is going down here."

"It's been top of mind for me too," Colin added. "Time and again on my deployments we would see clusters of crimes or action at a crossroads. We were always looking for intersections.

Swede nodded. "We did the same. Those clusters of activities were always key." He folded his arms, a frown marring his brow. "You think Eagle Rock is an intersection for this mob?"

Summer's stomach cramped as she covered the wound on Colin's arm.

"I'm wondering if the traffickers are trying new routes," Colin said. "Maybe there was a reason they had to come through. I'll ask Tyler to take a better look at weather or other crimes that happened around the day Autumn escaped."

"I'll go back and do the same search through our databases," Swede said. "Stay in touch." He walked out.

Their conversation had Summer's mind churning as well. About the kidnapping, about being flushed out of the witness protection house, and about how her testimony would go. "I feel so inadequate to this task," she admitted.

Colin checked his bandage. "Feels like you did

well enough to me. If teaching doesn't work out there's always nursing."

"Ha ha," she said, packing up the first aid kit without looking at him. "Despite everything I still *want* to teach. And I still want to teach those kids who are at risk."

"Then we'll make sure you get through this so you can do that." He stood up, putting his chest within kissing distance.

Her mind started counting the scars as she'd done last night, even as her body urged her to kiss him and put the last hour behind them.

Would it be so horrible to ask for a kiss, she wondered. "Take me to bed, Colin."

"What?" His gaze tangled with her reflection in the mirror.

"You heard me." She slid her palms over his chest. "I'll mind your bandage if you mind mine."

"To hell with my bandage."

He boosted her up into his arms and carried her to the bed, lavishing her with kisses. The second time proved the theory of practice making perfect.

THEY SETTLED into a comfortable routine over the next few days that were delightfully uneventful. Her stitches came out and his arm started to heal. They shared meals and long walks and under it all, she came to terms with the fact that she'd soon have to face her sister's kidnappers in court.

One morning she woke up in a fit of anxiety and fled the room. She just couldn't lean on Colin for one more thing. Despite the awareness that one of Hank's men was nearby, she didn't have the courage to sit by a window in the dining room. Tucked back against the wall at a table as close to the kitchen as possible, she thought about the man she'd left in bed upstairs. Mistake or blessing, it was hard to know how to classify her time with Colin.

Did it even need to be decided?

She wasn't into one night stands or casual flings and while her body would gladly take him anytime, her heart was growing too attached, longing for something more serious. Something long term. A ridiculous hope, all things considered. He had a career protecting people and she had math classes to teach.

The constant attacks were probably messing with her head. With a cup of coffee in hand, she strolled through the front room of the bed and breakfast. On a sideboard she found a notepad and pen available for guest use. Taking both back to the little table, she sat down to write a letter to her sister.

She didn't doubt Colin's ability to keep her alive, but just in case, she wanted to make sure to leave something for her sister. Assuming her sister was found.

Dear Autumn,

You need to know first and foremost I love you. I am so sorry for everything you've gone through. I feel responsible for your abduction because I was warned not to interfere when the gang was recruiting one of my students. I had no idea they would hurt me by taking you.

You were so brave creating your own escape. So strong to have survived an ordeal I cannot even fathom. These words are probably no comfort to you but I couldn't take the chance that you wouldn't know all of this.

I love you so much. If you ever want or need anything from me, I'll be there.

Always,

Summer

Ruby found an envelope and stamp and offered to post the letter for her. Summer addressed it to the U.S. Attorney's office in Helena and added a note for Hamilton to pass it along to Autumn.

She was just sitting down again when Colin walked in. The man stole her breath, and a warm flush flowed over her skin at the memory of his touch.

"I'm glad to find you here," he said. He leaned down and kissed her cheek.

"You were worried. Sorry." She should've left him a note.

"Let's just say nothing about your case has been predictable." He sat down across from her and accepted a cup of coffee.

The heat in his eyes gave her another thrill. It was nice being wanted. Nicer still to be valued. He made her feel like a treasure. Special. How odd that it was a stranger who'd given her what she'd craved all her life.

"How is your arm?" she asked, pointing to the edge of the fresh bandage showing under the sleeve of his shirt.

"I'm good." He bobbed his eyebrows. "Seems laughter isn't the only best medicine around."

She was grateful her skin didn't reveal her every disquieting thought. But another hot gaze told her he knew. She hid a responding smile behind her cup. "So what do we do now?"

"I just got off the phone with Tyler," he reported. "Hamilton is hoping to speak with you later today at Hank's office.

Her stomach rolled and she set the cup aside. "I just wrote a letter to my sister hoping Hamilton could deliver it to her."

"You've given up on speaking to her directly?" he asked.

"Not giving up…"

"You're taking precautions," he said. His gaze clouded, the warmth gone.

"And now I've offended you."

His stared into his coffee.

She wondered if he found any answers there.

Neither her coffee nor the tea that followed had been as enlightening as she'd hoped.

At last he looked up met her gaze. "Not offended, no. I get it." He leaned back in his chair. "I will get you through this. You don't have to believe me for it to be true. But I also understand precautions. Sometimes writing it down is the only way to get the words out the right way."

"I've said similar things to my students," she said with a smile.

Ruby set a plate of pancakes and bacon in front of Colin and he dug in.

"I'm going to get some air," she said. For some reason, sitting here pretending life was normal wasn't working for her.

"I'll come with you," he said, rising.

"No." It wasn't him, it was her. "Eat. I'll be fine."

"Summer."

"Colin." She mimicked his tone. "I'm going to sit on the porch with my tea and my mood and deal. Take your time."

She knew he didn't like it, but she was a grown woman and she needed a breather from all the emotions and turmoil swirling through her system. Autumn, the case, and the bodyguard she was too close to were starting to overwhelm her.

Outside, the fresh air and sunshine settled her just enough. She set her mug on the rail and stared up into the mountains, her mind on her sister.

When a board creaked, she didn't turn around, certain it was Colin.

She was wrong.

~

"Shit!" Colin said. He paced back and forth across Hank Patterson's kitchen. "He took her right out from under my nose. I know better than this."

It had been the longest twenty minutes of his life, giving Summer her space outside. Then he'd gone after her and found only her cup of unfinished tea. Though he'd searched the area and called Hank immediately, there weren't any obvious leads, no sign of a struggle.

Hank tried to calm him down. "You're not the first one who's been fooled on a case. The Native Mob has hired some very talented people," he said.

"So what do we do about it?" Colin demanded. "I can't leave her out there. I won't fail her." He pushed a hand through his hair and paced back and forth across the back porch.

He felt absolutely miserable. She was his responsibility and so much more. Somehow in their short time together he'd found a woman who believed he was worth something. Together there was something bright and hopeful between them and he'd let down his guard for twenty short minutes and she'd disappeared.

She hadn't walked off on her own. Not at this point, not after everything they'd shared. She was committed to seeing Autumn's kidnappers sent to jail for their crimes.

"I've put Joe and Six on it," Hank said. "They can track anyone through these mountains. Swede is working with Tyler to analyze anything we can get from security cameras around town. Whoever took her might be skilled at hiding, but we will prevail."

How many times had Colin delivered similar assurances to a client?

Hank snapped his fingers. "Work with me," he barked. "Tell me everything you know about Summer. Will she panic or will she keep her head? Does she know how to leave a trail?"

Colin thought about what he'd learned about Summer in the short time they'd been together. "She has good wilderness skills," he said. "She won't lose her head and I bet anything she's already leaving us a trail."

"All right." Hank nodded to the men around him. "Let's get out there and find that trail."

CHAPTER 9

SUMMER WAS furious with herself and for the man
dragging her away from Eagle Rock. The man she
and Colin called Tony has seized her and dumped
her into a car before she could even scream. He'd
driven out of town toward the mountains and pulled
over, leaving the car on the shoulder. Now they were
hiking to who-knew-where. Through a break in the
trees she caught a glimpse of another man further up
the hill waiting by what looked like two four-wheeler
all-terrain vehicles. That didn't bode well for her.

She could *not* let them get her on that machine or
no one would find her again. She'd done what she
could to be awkward and slow and leave a trail, but
there was no guarantee anyone would stumble
across it.

"Why not just kill me now?" She stopped where

the thick trunk of a tree blocked her from the waiting man's sight.

"Move it," Tony barked.

She started to move and then plopped right down to the ground. "No. You're just going to kill me," she complained while she rooted around for a stick or rock to use against him. "I'm tired. Do it now and spare me a twisted ankle in the process."

"I should." Tony pulled out his gun. "A few holes in the right places won't reduce your price."

"What?" He couldn't mean that.

"Oh, you didn't get the memo?" Tony bent close, hands braced on his knees and his lip curled up in a snarl. "I'm supposed to take you alive as restitution for your bitch sister."

Her hand had found a rock and she gripped it hard as she lunged at him, landing an uppercut to his jaw. He fell back and she kept on going, knocking away the gun and landing two more good blows before he bucked her off of him.

She rolled down the slope and got to her feet. Dizzy and disoriented, she looked around. She had to get back to the road and find some help. Tony fired at her, the bullet cracking a small branch near her shoulder. Jerking out of the way, she lost her footing and went sliding again.

Right into a big German shepherd and his bigger handler.

"Six, go!" The dog raced up the slope while the

man gave her a hand up. "I'm Joe," he said. "You okay?"

"Summer," she said. "And I'm much better now. Thanks." An engine sounded. "The second man," she said in a hurry. "Further up. He had two four-wheelers."

Joe gave a solemn nod. "Hank is down near the road. Can you make it?"

She opened her mouth to assure him she'd be fine when a screech preceded a falling body. Tony tumbled by in slow motion, unable to arrest his fall because his hands and feet were tied.

"That first step's a doozy."

She looked up into Colin's bloodthirsty face and scrambled up the hill, throwing herself into his arms. "I'm so sorry!" His hands flitted over her, checking for injuries. "I'm fine," she said. "Just an idiot for walking out that way."

"No. Forget it. Thank God you're okay."

He pulled her into a tight hug and she clung like a burr. All around them Joe and the dog and other men she didn't know were dealing with Tony and the second man.

"Summer, I've never been so terrified. Not since..." He held her close kissed her face all over, careful of the fresh scrapes and scratches.

"Come on. That can't be true. You were chased by a drone in a hotel once." She wanted to lighten the mood, unwilling to let him slide back into the mire of those dark memories when he'd been a prisoner.

"I haven't," he insisted. "When I was a prisoner it was all about me. All about getting back and getting out the truth about the soldiers I lost." He shook his head. "This time all I worried about was what they would put you through if I didn't get here in time. Without Hank and his men I might not have found you. That—" His voice cracked. "That was true terror."

His words undid her. "You saved me. Again. Always it seems. I'm so happy to see you." She tried to smile, to reassure him, but it felt all watery and wrong. "I wasn't looking forward to spending the night with that jerk and his pal."

He kissed her gently. "Do you want another body-guard to take over your case?"

The idea was so absurd she laughed and heads turned their way. "They think I'm hysterical."

"Are you?" he asked, concerned.

"No." She gripped his shoulders, waiting until he met her gaze. "There is no replacing you," she said. "You're stuck with me, mister."

He took a deep breath, looking way more relieved than he should. "This was my mistake," she said. "I'm the one who insisted on having space at the wrong time."

"No, no," he protested. "I let the line get blurred."

"Can we argue about it later and kiss more right now?"

He obliged her with another sweet kiss before they resumed the walk down to the road. "Whether or not we argue, we can't stay at Ruby's. Patterson has a team lined up to escort us to a hotel closer to Helena. We'll be safe there until you testify."

"Thank you, Colin. For everything." Oh, she had it bad, she was so crazy in love with this man. Her breath fluttered in and out of her chest. Relief. Fury. Relief. Hope. And more relief.

Though it was silly and girly, she latched onto Colin and wouldn't let go. She'd fallen hard and fast for a man who'd thought his past and his scars made him unlovable. She knew better, because she was the one who loved him. Now she just had to sort out if or when she should tell him.

Definitely now. Probably never. The small voice of logic in her head argued with her heart.

How would Colin react? Would he blame her feelings on her circumstances and the case?

She gazed up into his face and knew that no matter when or where, she would love this man. His eyes were stone cold as he glared at Tony who was whining about rights and misunderstandings.

"If he knows the name of the mole in the U.S. Attorney's office, Hank and the sheriff will know it soon enough," Colin said.

His gaze fell to her and everything inside her shifted, deepening under the intensity blazing in his eyes. The forceful expression almost knocked her back. Instead she pressed closer. Was she reading too much into the way he fussed over her? Rubbing her cheek to his shoulder, the words were right there on the tip of her tongue.

I love you.

Three small words she wanted so desperately to give him. Not because he'd chased down Tony and trussed him up like goose. Her heart hadn't tumbled at his feet over any one thing, it was the culmination of discovering someone who was messed up in his own ways and so damn steady and reliable in spite of his weaknesses.

She didn't even need to hear his response. She wanted to give them those words, give him her heart, no matter what he did with the information. Her stomach fluttered. It was the strangest place for a life-altering epiphany. "Colin…"

Swede walked up. "I'll give you guys a lift back," he said. "Hank and the sheriff can deal with Tony and his pal. We'll cover you to Helena."

The moment broke like a popped balloon and she kept her feelings to herself on the ride back into town. Swede dropped them at the door of the bed and breakfast so they could pack and pick up Colin's car for the drive to Helena.

"The first thing I'm doing when we get to the hotel is taking a long hot shower," she said as she took a minute to brush the leaves out of her hair and pull it back in a messy bun.

"With me?" he asked, hopefully.

"I'd like that," she admitted. "Will you kiss me again?"

"I'd like that." He sidled over and rested his hands gently on her hips. Then his lips were on hers, soft and warm and reassuring. It was a beautiful testament to survival, a lovely affirmation of life despite the persistent threats. And it was damn hard to break away so they could make the necessary drive to Helena.

"It's almost over," he said when they arrived at the hotel.

The man had a knack for sensing her distress. The trial was a necessity, but she wasn't looking forward to it at all. She could go the rest of her life without seeing the men who'd taken her sister. Not to mention, once Hamilton was done with her, Colin would be reassigned. Where would that leave them? She'd been a fool for falling in love with him, but she just couldn't regret a minute of her time with him.

"The security team has been briefed and is on high alert," Colin was saying. "Between them, Hank's guys and me, no one else will get to you."

"I believe you," she said. "If I hadn't been so irritable and stubborn no one would have gotten to me in Eagle Rock."

"Two of us were stubborn," Colin said. "I should

have come up with a safe way for you to have some space. I'm sorry, Summer. So damned sorry."

"Please stop apologizing," she begged. "Mistakes are just part of this thing we call life." She chewed on her lip as she stared through the glass doors into the lobby. "I've been wondering," she began.

"If you'll ever get to see Autumn," he finished for her.

"You're a mind reader," she joked.

"Not a big stretch," he said. "I know what she means to you. When you speak with Hamilton, just ask her outright what she knows about Autumn. I'm sure she's doing everything possible to find her and keep the case on track." He reached over and pulled her in for a fast kiss. "Let's get checked in," he said. "Then we can get that shower."

She laughed when he wagged his eyebrows. "Deal."

"Do you think there's any way to put an end to this for good?" she asked hours later when they were snuggled on the bed, mostly dry, and completely sated.

"I doubt it," he said. "Criminals do their thing. That isn't going to change."

"I suppose not. It's just so frustrating to have the tribes fighting against each other. Human trafficking is bad enough." She sat up a little and combed her fingers through her hair, plaiting it. "I know historically different tribes did terrible things to protect land and resources. These days should be different. Haven't we grown at all as a people?"

Restless, she stalked to the window and back, sitting next to his hip. "We should be better to each other." She trailed her finger down the jagged scar on his side. "Things like this should never happen again."

He sighed and pressed her hand flat against the scar, holding her still. "This was war, honey. People will never be perfect. Selfish people exist. Undereducated people exist. People who crave power exist. And because of that here we are."

"I'm not sure I like your philosophy, Mr. Psychology today." When he smiled her tension eased. She dragged her hands up over his chest, skimming the scars there. "So are we just supposed to keep being good people and a bad world?"

"I'm afraid that's about all I've got. Especially when you're touching me." He brought her lips to his for a lingering kiss.

"*Mmm.*" She nuzzled his neck, nipped his jaw. "You've got much more than that."

"I'm surprised you think so," he said. "You were kidnapped on my watch."

"Don't you dare feel guilty about that," she insisted. "No matter which one of us was more stubborn, Tony was determined and sneaky. "He was watching for that opening. If we're supposed to be good people in a bad world, then he was just doing his job being a bad person in a really nice town."

Fortunately, she was able to distract him with more kisses, silencing tomorrow's worries for just a little longer.

But sleep was elusive once the lights were out and Colin, being his observant self, sensed it. "Are you afraid to stand up in court and tell your side of the story?" he asked.

"A little," she confessed. "I'm definitely not looking forward to admitting in court how my actions led to them seizing my sister."

"Check that with Hamilton," he said. "She may not need to go there and the defense definitely won't want to talk about that. If you have concerns, speak up in the prep tomorrow. We won't leave until you're confident."

Maybe some of his innate confidence would rub off on her after spending all this time with him. "I will," she said. "I don't have anything to hide and after Tony's last hurrah, I will not stay silent. They can try all they want, I won't let them make me a victim."

"That's my girl." He curled his body around hers, one hand stroking her hair. "I doubt they will keep trying. They've thrown around a lot of money and manpower stop the trial and failed. At this point I'd be surprised if the kidnappers survive long enough to attend their sentencing."

That snapped her back to fully awake. How had it never occurred to her that those men would be killed for their crimes? She twisted to face Colin. "What do you mean?"

"The mob can't let them live if there's a chance they'll expose more of the operation."

"What kind of person am I if I don't want them to get off easy but I don't want them to die either?"

"You're you." He bumped his nose to hers. "The kind of person who believes people are inherently good."

"That doesn't sound like much of a compliment," she grumbled.

"Oh, but it is," he said. "Without you, I would've happily forgotten about some of the good parts of me."

He pulled her close. "Sleep, now. All you have to do is tell the truth and let Justice do her thing."

CHAPTER 10

On the day of the trial, Colin applied every tactic he'd learned in his professional training to hide his nerves from Summer. The last thing she needed was for him to make her more anxious while they waited for the proceedings to begin. It had felt like running a gauntlet, but they made it inside the courthouse without taking fire. He had wanted a tank, an armed escort, and riot shields and bulletproof vests for everyone. The prosecution had wanted her to walk in without any extra precautions, just to make a point. He wasn't about to take that risk after working so hard to keep her alive.

Thanks to Hank, they reached a compromise, with the Brotherhood Protectors offering a motorcade escort and additional manpower for Summer's protection.

After a brief meeting with Hamilton, they entered

the courtroom and bided their time until the U.S. Attorney called Summer to the stand. Her fingers tightened around his hand just a moment and then she stood. Regal as a queen, she passed the kidnappers on her way to the witness box, ignoring them as Hamilton suggested. She raised her right hand and in a tone laced with steel, she swore to tell the truth.

With quiet, calm dignity she relayed the events of the day her sister had disappeared. When asked, she courageously identified the men in the courtroom, the defendants, as the men responsible for shoving her sister into the bed of a pickup truck and driving away.

When it was time for the cross examination, the defense attorney did little more than verify her relationship to Autumn. It was as if everyone in the courtroom knew the case was open-and-shut.

Her poise and grace under pressure astounded him. He was so damn proud of her and honored to have played even a small part in getting her here. Despite how well she was managing, his palms were sweating. He wanted this to be over and behind her almost as much as he wanted to be able to stay with her. As a lover and as a partner. Not solely as her bodyguard.

Last night while Summer slept, he'd exchanged text messages with Tyler. The agency was keeping him assigned to her for the next six months due to the likelihood of retribution.

He supposed the timing would fluctuate based on how the prosecution chose to pursue the Native Mob. As serious as that was he would happily stand guard, but he was more concerned with *her*. When could she get back to teaching school and fulfilling her passion? When would she walk down the street again without fear?

Her testimony complete, she was dismissed from the witness stand. Her gaze locked with his and she held her head high as she returned to her seat next to him. He expected Hamilton to rest the case but she didn't.

"We have one more witness, your honor. Autumn Curley will testify from a secure location."

Summer's tensed and she clutched his hand with both of hers. "They found her?" she whispered. "Did you know? Is she okay?"

"*Shh.*" He shook his head and tucked her under his arm. Her body quivered with the emotions rioting through her. "They obviously didn't share to better protect her," he murmured at her ear. "Hang in there."

The defense attorney blustered, but after a brief approach to the bench, the protests were settled.

At Hamilton's nod, a flat panel television was wheeled in to face the jury. The screen flickered to life and Autumn's face appeared. Beside him Summer was rigid, her breath ragged as she fought to keep quiet. The younger Curley sister delivered her testimony with the same cool demeanor as

Summer had done. Prompted by Hamilton's expert questions, Autumn gave a detailed chronological account of the kidnapping and every harrowing abuse and humiliation that followed while she was a captive.

Beside him, tears flowed unchecked down her Summer's cheeks as one ugly detail after another came to light. Even if Summer reconciled with her sister, he feared she'd never forgive herself. She deserved so much more than a life shadowed by guilt and grief.

Finally, once the defense declined the opportunity to cross examine, the ordeal was over. A bailiff ushered them out of the courtroom, down one floor, and into a small conference room with an oval table and a dozen chairs. A beverage cart was set up with chilled water, coffee, and a pot of hot water for tea.

"Do you think they'll give us a few minutes to talk here?" she asked. "I really want to see her. I hope she'll let me give her a hug."

"All we can do is wait and see." There was no guarantee Autumn was even in this building, but he wasn't about to dash her hope. He fixed her a cup of tea while she paced, wondering what Hamilton had in mind.

"The agency has extended my assignment with you," he said, handing her the tea.

She nodded absently, her dark brown eyes were still glossy from her earlier tears. With the cup in her hands, she returned to the window, sipping the hot liquid carefully.

"I'll have to start looking for work," she said.

He shoved his hands into his pockets. "I assumed you'd want to go back to the reservation and the school where you taught before."

"I don't think so." She set aside her cup and vigorously tugged out the pins holding up her hair until it tumbled down past her shoulders. "I'm not sure I'll ever feel safe there again. Even with you nearby."

She had to know he'd never let anyone hurt her. "You can't let violence or trauma dictate your choices," he reminded her. "Besides I'll be there."

"For how long?"

That was a tricky question considering everything that was rolling through his head. "For as long as you need me," he vowed. Forever, if the next few minutes went according to plan.

"What about your career and your preference for all things less remote than where I teach on the reservation?"

"Sweetheart if I have learned anything in these last two weeks it's that I love you. I can always find a new career but I cannot live without *you*."

Her lips parted, clearly shocked by his declaration. The door swung open and Hamilton walked in before she could respond. His heart kicked in protest that any decisions about their future would have to wait a little longer.

"Summer you were amazing. Thank you. I don't think the jury will be long in reaching a guilty verdict." She turned to Colin. "Your agency promised your cooperation with the witness tampering charges."

"My pleasure," he said. "Whatever you need, count on me. This has to be stopped."

"I agree. We've taken big steps in the right direction today," Hamilton said with confidence.

"When can I see my sister?" Summer asked. "Where did you find her?"

Uncertainty rushed over Hamilton's face. "Well, that was the delay," the U.S. Attorney said. "I'd planned for a visit between you and your sister right here. But she disappeared again."

"What?" He and Summer said in unison.

"She wasn't taken," Hamilton assured them. "Her protective custody warned me they thought she was plotting an escape on her own terms."

"And she did," Summer said, clearly dejected.

"It seems so."

"Will that jeopardize your second case?" he asked Hamilton.

"No," replied Hamilton. She reached over and patted Summer's shoulder. "But it makes me sad that the two of you haven't seen each other."

"One thing you can count on with my little sister is she's headstrong."

He wrapped Summer in his arms and just held

her for a minute. "And she's capable," he reminded her. He'd heard enough Curley sister stories to be confident of that much. "We'll get Tyler on her trail," he added. He wanted to be her everything, but he knew how important her family ties were. If there was any way to reunite the Curley sisters, he would make sure it happened.

The prosecutor walked out and Colin continued to hold her, wondering how to resume their more personal conversation. "I have a surprise for you," he said, kissing the top of her head.

She looked up at him, a small frown pleating her eyebrows. "Here?"

He stepped toward the corner where he'd asked the bailiff to stash his gift and lifted the oversized box onto the table. "Open it."

"Looks a little big for an engagement ring," she said, wariness in her dark eyes.

Did that mean she'd been hoping for a proposal? He'd sure been hoping to give her one, if not here today, then soon.

With maddening slowness, she untied the ribbon and raised the lid. Recognizing the logo on the tissue paper, excitement lit her up. She rushed to pull out the fluffy white robe, clutching it close and nuzzling it to her cheek.

"Colin, you're the best!"

"I told you I'd hook you up," he said. "Think you can enjoy it?"

"To the fullest." Still holding the robe, she threw her arms around him and kissed him soundly. "I love you, Colin Hazard."

For several minutes he savored her kisses, each one more precious than the last. "Is it too soon to propose?"

"Ask and find out," she dared.

Adoring her sassy side, he dropped to one knee. "Summer Curley, will you make me the happiest man alive and be my wife?" Her smile was as bright and blinding and wonderful as sunlight. "I promise to love and cherish you every day of my life, whether conditions are fluffy or rough."

Laughing, she perched on his knee and peppered his face with kisses.

"Is that a yes?"

"Definitely. I love you. Yes, I'll marry you. I'll be yours. Forever. You're the treasure I didn't know to wish for."

Standing, they packed the robe back into the box and walked out of the courthouse hand in hand. For the first time in years, his heart felt whole, all the tattered edges of his soul mended. She'd done that. At his car he hesitated. "You need a ring," he said.

"I do," she replied with a cheeky grin.

"Left to my own devices, you'll wind up with something well-above average." It was only fair to warn her.

Her eyes twinkled. "Promise?"

He couldn't wait to surprise her, to spoil her, to give her everything her heart desired for the rest of her days. "I do."

Wherever they landed, between his career and hers, in posh hotels or rural schools, Colin was confident they were going to create a beautiful life.

Guardian Agency ~ Brotherhood Protectors crossover novels

Dylan

Mike

Nathan

Dallas

Unknown Identities Series

Bulletproof

Double Vision

Sandman

Death-Trap Date

Unknown Identities - Brotherhood Protectors crossover novellas:

Moving Target

Lost Signal

Off The Radar

Escape Club Heroes Series

Escape Club, prequel

Safe In His Sight

A Stranger She Can Trust

Escape Club: Justice, novella

Escape Club: Sabotage, novella

Protecting Her Secret Son

Braving The Heat

More Romantic Suspense

Runaway Secret

His Soldier Under Siege (February 2020)

Colton Family Showdown

A Soldier's Honor

Colton P.I. Protector

Killer Colton Christmas

Knight Traveler Series, paranormal romance

Heart of Time, prequel

Timeless Vision

An Heirloom Amber, novella

Timeless Changes

The Memory Key, novella

Timeless Light

Matchmaker Series, paranormal romance

The Matchmaker's Mark

The Matchmaker's Curse

The Bodyguard's Vow

ABOUT REGAN BLACK

Regan Black, a USA Today and internationally best-selling author, writes award-winning, action-packed romances featuring kick-butt heroines and the sexy heroes who fall in love with them. Raised in the Midwest and California, she and her family and two adorably arrogant cats now reside in the South Carolina Lowcountry where the rich blend of legend, romance, and history fuels her imagination.

For early access to new book releases, exclusive prizes, and much more, subscribe to the monthly newsletter at ReganBlack.com/perks.

Keep up with Regan online:
www.ReganBlack.com
Facebook
Twitter
Instagram

facebook.com/ReganBlack.fans
twitter.com/ReganBlack
instagram.com/reganblackauthor

ORIGINAL BROTHERHOOD
PROTECTORS SERIES

BY ELLE JAMES

ABOUT ELLE JAMES

ELLE JAMES also writing as MYLA JACKSON is a *New York Times* and *USA Today* Bestselling author of books including cowboys, intrigues and paranormal adventures that keep her readers on the edges of their seats. With over eighty works in a variety of sub-genres and lengths she has published with Harlequin, Samhain, Ellora's Cave, Kensington, Cleis Press, and Avon. When she's not at her computer, she's traveling, snow skiing, boating, or riding her ATV, dreaming up new stories. Learn more about Elle James at www.ellejames.com

Website | Facebook | Twitter | GoodReads | Newsletter | BookBub | Amazon

Follow Elle!
www.ellejames.com
ellejames@ellejames.com

facebook.com/ellejamesauthor

twitter.com/ElleJamesAuthor